FALLING FOR HOME

KIM SMART

Life doesn't happen to us, it happens with us and I am grateful to have my family to do life with. Thanks for all your support and enthusiasm, listening to my stories and loving my characters.

CONTENTS

CHAPTER 1

"Geez Jesse, honey, did you roll in the cow pile before you shoveled it?" Yvette Davies smiled at her handsome son standing in the doorway. Straw dust swarmed like gnats in the late afternoon sunrays. She playfully wrinkled her nose at the all-to-familiar scent of cattle waste. The faint voice of her late father-in-law whispered his favorite phrase in her head, "Ah, the sweet smell of money."

Dried Badlands clay caked his jeans and boots as he stepped into her prized mudroom; the room she fought for when the architect drew up their dream home plans after a few exceptional years. Living and raising a family in the hundred-year-old Davies family farmhouse carried a certain stereotypical, oppressed, ultra-conservative image of ranch-life tradition. Ample opportunities to develop home-maintenance skills lived in that house. For Yvette and Dan Davies, living, riding, working the land and cattle, and raising their family on Buffalo Ridge was all they needed. They worked hard over the years. They rewarded themselves with the new house.

Jesse reached down to pull off his crusty work boots and looked up at Yvette; a smile crossed his speckled face, a mixture of mud and freckles. "Of course I did Ma. You guys always told me I was the best manure-wrangler you ever saw, and I didn't want to disappoint."

Yvette and Dan welcomed four beautiful babies into their Buffalo Ridge clan. As the youngest of four, Jesse inherited some unique challenges. All the children were excellent students and athletically inclined. Jesse's siblings were accomplished. He struggled to be exceptional at something.

Wrangling manure was his trademark. He became the butt of a family joke as a young boy trying to keep up with his older siblings. Yvette realized that today, that joke would fit squarely within the bullying category. "Family. We could certainly be thoughtless," she chastised herself. But the Davies family mantra was one of overcoming all the elements. They never let bad weather or manure get them down.

The joke started when Jesse was seven. Five years younger than his next oldest sibling, Stella, Jesse worked hard to be as good as the older kids. Practicing baseball in the yard was one of the family's favorite spring activities. It was important in the Davies family to be a standout in sports. Stella, at twelve, was a scrappy basketball player on the grade school team and a barrel-racing prodigy. At fourteen, Chance was riding broncos and roping, wrestled with the varsity team, and could have been in the stand-up comedy hall of fame. He would rather tell jokes than pay attention in the classroom any day. Already the girls were ringing the house phone, hoping to hear Chance answer before quickly hanging up, hoping to be unidentifiable. The oldest son, Steve, left soon after for college. A scholarship to rope on the rodeo team was his; he would be on the roping team. He had already set several state records in track and football and enjoyed a good showing in rodeo roping. As an excellent student, he set the bar high for the rest of the Davies kids. Townspeople and family alike constantly compared Jesse to his exceptional siblings. Ranking of the children by teachers in the small-town school was one of the biggest challenges to overcome, second only to the constant pressure of his siblings.

On that fateful day, Chance hit a foul ball toward the feed-lot. Steve yelled to Jesse to catch it so they could win the game. Jesse didn't like baseball, didn't watch it on TV, and didn't know, or care about, the actual rules of the game. Jesse simply wanted to be a worthy teammate for his big brother Steve. He did what he was told. He took off after that ball, using all his speed and agility to get under it. The weathered boards of the corral fence appeared before he could swerve to avoid them. He leaped up to catch the ball and toppled into a pile of manure. When he emerged, he wore a grin and held the ball in his stinky greased glove. Dung clung to him as he stood. The entire family laughed at him. "Look Ma!" Chance yelled. "You're raising a manure-wrangler now." They crowned Jesse the manure wrangler, a name that passed for all but Jesse. The sting was still there for him.

Chance put Jesse down at every opportunity. He was the class clown and his joke was not a compliment; he never intended it to be. Jesse had to stay outside until he washed with the garden hose and stripped off his filthy clothes. He stunk like something that belonged in the barn. He didn't know, until that day, that a foul ball was a dead ball. Someone should have told him the rules. He hated his siblings for not telling him.

Reading was his passion, as was his horse, Motor. Motor had one gear: slow and reliable. That was Jesse's preference. Motor was predictable and safe. Jesse held his emotions close and colored inside the lines.

"Ah Jess, you never disappoint." Yvette looked directly at her son. These were more than merely reassuring words of a mother. She was proud of the man her son was becoming. "Get out of those nasty clothes and shower. Kerry will stand you up, as rightly she should, if you don't show up on time and with a shine."

Yvette handed him a towel and waived her hand in the air

as if to shoo him into action. She wanted him to take his work clothes off and toss them in the wash.

Yvette, more than anyone in the family, saw Jesse for the wonderfully unique man he was becoming. She paused as she walked back to the kitchen. Her eyes fell on the yard outside the window. Her mind wandered back to those days when the family played in the yard. In the winter they plowed snow into tall mounds for sledding. In spring and summer they played baseball or touch football. From this vantage point, she saw Jesse trying to fit in yet standing out like salt against pepper. Her hands rested on her chest, soothing her mother's regret. She could have protected his tender emotions better. She gently shook her head to send the image back to the past. We all need to move forward doing the best we can do, she told herself.

The sweet smell of onions sautéing beckoned her back to the kitchen where she was preparing dinner. She looked toward the driveway of the shop, hoping to see Dan's truck. After all these years, she still worried about him. She stirred the vegetables in the pan, sprinkled in cumin and garlic powder. She kept her hands busy paring an apple and slicing a banana for the salad.

Jesse tugged off his boots and drew his long legs out of his jeans. At twenty, he still had the body of a teenager with long, lean limbs and little muscle definition. He was strong enough but lacked the typical muscular dark Davies physique, chick magnets with ease in conversation and a glowing love for life. Jesse was more pale, less beefy, more introverted and skeptical about life. He hid in books and under headphones.

Jesse was the smartest of the kids; at least that's what his mother and his test scores said. "College material," the guidance counselor told him. But he was not interested. His mind was always working. He couldn't make it stop. So he found it necessary to ground himself in physical labor. Yes, he got the best grades and was at the top of the Davies heap in high school, with Stella coming in a close second. He missed Stella. She was his closest friend, besides Kerry.

Stella went off to Arizona to find herself, and cattle. Toiling in physical labor grounded Stella in the same way it did for Jesse. School was stifling. They longed for the solitude of wide-open space, dirt on their hands and fresh air in their lungs. Jesse hadn't seen her since her class reunion two summers before. Too much time had passed. She was Stella, the cowboy, like some super hero persona. Sleeping under the stars, unplugged from social media most of the time, defined her. He sent her messages. She responded when she could. Maybe Jesse could visit her when he got a break, whenever that was. Like most things in his life, Jesse overanalyzed and frequently ascribed a fatal ending to the conundrum before him.

Jesse's tough cowboy edge softened with Kerry around. He was relaxed, yet alert to her kind heart and curious mind. She was a sophomore and he a senior when they started dating. It started with an invitation to a dance. His friends all had dates and someone suggested he ask Kerry. They became an exclusive dating couple that night. Even after he graduated they continued to date. He had now been to six proms. Awkward. Heading to college with her dreams in tow was Kerry's idea of bliss. He loved her company and would miss her. He wasn't interested in finding someone else.

Exploring the Badlands was one of their favorite things to do. The sprawling wild land rested at the foot of Buffalo Ridge Ranch. They rode in those parts year-round, when time allowed. During those rides they witnessed the unrestrained wildlife. One day they witnessed a Bison calving. More than once on a spring ride mating rattlesnakes interrupted their ride. Several prairie dog towns peppered the basin floor. Visiting those places and watching the prairie dogs poke their pointed little noses in the air was entertaining.

He didn't understand why, but Kerry was his ever-faithful girlfriend who promised to stick by his side come hell or high water. Here on Buffalo Ridge Ranch, either was possible. In fact, hell came summer after summer in the form of high winds, brush fires and day after day of one- hundred-degree plus heat and humidity. High water arrived every spring when the snow melted onto the hard-packed skin of the Badlands where it became clay, stickier than quicksand, and creeks flooded, knocking out bridges, fencing, and roads.

Jesse often wondered why anyone would homestead, and then stay, in this miserable country. Then he witnessed the bold lightening reach down from a grey stormy sky toward the Badlands, illuminating the dramatic shapes nature built there over the centuries. And on a crisp winter night when the full moon lit the snow-covered valley toward town where streetlights danced in the ice fog, he stared with disbelief that such a beautiful place could exist. Some days, most days in fact, there was no place that he would rather be.

These days he questioned that. Going to college may be what he needed. The problem, as he saw it, was that he had no interest in studying business or agriculture. Everything he needed to know about running a ranch he learned from his parents. He didn't see himself going anywhere except maybe down the road to his own place. Someday, maybe.

Smelling fresh like Irish Spring soap, Jesse got dressed and cleaned out his truck. He grabbed an old t-shirt and brushed out the dust. Jesse tossed the empty soda and water bottles in the trash and got behind the wheel. He looked behind him to ensure his going-away gift lay there. He hoped he wouldn't chicken out and not give it to her. This was her night. Letting Kerry enjoy her last night in town was his priority. Giving her this gift was selfish on his part. He wanted her to take a piece of him with her. It was there, wrapped in bright pink paper with a silver bow. It reminded him of her at the prom. She was so beautiful. A real prize.

Summer's end brought the town's annual harvest celebration. Tonight was the last night to hang with friends before

Kerry left for school. Kissing and close dancing were in the forecast.

He loved having her close. It calmed him. Made him feel special. He would miss these times with her. Sometimes he worried they, or at least he, had taken for granted the closeness of their community and their home. It was comforting to know she planned to come home at Christmas. Until then, her focus was on school. It was hard, but they agreed to only talk on Sundays. Dreading the time apart, Jesse told Kerry he would miss her but wanted her to succeed. She deserved that. He wasn't going anywhere. He feared she would leave him in the dust after meeting college guys.

Starting at an early age, Kerry's dream was to become a veterinarian. Her mother said she would scour the fields for sick and injured creatures and bring them to the house. Bandaging a stray cat's bloody paw or feeding a sickly pullet with an eyedropper was not uncommon for Kerry. Practicing in Buffalo Ridge was part of her dream. It had been a decade since the last veterinarian gave up residence here in this small town. Small towns are hard to survive if you have big ideas. These good old boys like it their way with money in the bank, boots on the ground and generations of homogeneity sharing know-how. Yeah, Buffalo Ridge isn't very diverse. It could be an uphill battle for Kerry but Jesse would do anything to see her succeed. Already he was thinking of places that would be suitable for a clinic. Jesse hoped to have one lined up when she was ready to establish her practice.

CHAPTER 2

*K*erry raced into the house, throwing off her waitress uniform as she bee-lined for her room. No time for a shower. It wouldn't be the first time she went out wearing the lingering scent of chicken-fried steak and splattered Thousand Island dressing. Nothing a little body spray wouldn't hide. She would not miss this summer job. Like so many tables this year, that last table was so demanding, lingering over their meal like it was a hundred-dollar a plate at a five-star restaurant with a tip reserved for a carhop. She, like most of the small town's residents, appreciated the tourists for the revenue they brought in the summer but boy, could they be difficult and so ungrateful.

"Kerry, can I do anything to help you get ready?" Susan had already helped her cull the essentials from her bedroom to take to college, pack her bags, her car, and wrote a list of essentials to pick up when she arrived in Brookstone. The University was Susan's alma mater, and she was excited that her daughter was going as far away for school as she could, while still keeping in-state scholarships and tuition rates. Unlike herself, though, Susan hoped that Kerry would stay and complete her education and move away from this God-forsaken country with its harsh winds and even harsher townspeople. Susan married a fourth-generation Braun and would have done anything not to return to this small town where people are small-minded. But, she fell in love and it was love and having a family that brought her back and kept her here. She did her best to fit in and make it work.

"Thanks, Mom. I've got it. Jesse will be here in…" A knock at the door interjected.

"Come on in Jess." Susan liked Jesse well enough. He was smart and polite and always good to her daughter. But he was here. In this small town with these small-minded people. She did not want to alienate her daughter, so she was nice to Jesse. Susan just wished he wasn't so committed to this town and his family's ranch. She was grateful that Kerry took her advice not to come home the first few months of school and not to hang on that dang phone night and day with him like she had done.

"Wow, you look so pretty, Kerry. You ready to go kick up some dust?" Jesse smiled at her as she strode into the front room, sporting tight jeans with sparkling patches on her tiny butt, a tooled leather belt circling her tinier waist and a glittery blue tank top shouting, "Taking on the world, one cowboy at a time."

Kerry and her girlfriends picked up these matching tank tops on a mid-summer girls' trip to the Cheyenne rodeo. The six girls were long-time schoolmates and friends. They played basketball, ran track and were in 4-H together. Kerry, Charlotte, and Kate were all in rodeo. Kerry and Whitney worked at The Buffalo Diner together the past three summers and Cathy was the nice girl who was friends with everyone. She was getting married at Christmas and the girls would all be her bridesmaids. Kerry was happy to have this to look forward to. Staying connected with these girls she loved was important to Kerry.

The tank top with the sparkling message drew a lot of attention from the guys in Cheyenne - especially Brandon, a fun-loving cowboy from Wyoming who was blowing up her phone with messages. She took her phone out of her back pocket. "Mom, will you put this on the charger for me? I want it ready to go for tomorrow."

She didn't need Jesse to know about Brandon. Nothing had happened, well, not much anyway.

"Thanks, babe. Do you mind if we run by The Buffalo on our way to the dance? JoAnn promised to have my last paycheck ready for me since I'm leaving tomorrow." Kerry needed every last dime to pay for schoolbooks and tuition. Her daddy worked hard farming and ranching but he wasn't well-to-do like the Davies, who had a rodeo stock business on the side. He paid the bills but Momma didn't get silk panties. That was his long-standing joke. If he ever had a successful crop that is the day Momma would get silk panties. Poor Mom. Kerry knew she longed for more but kept the peace because she loved her family.

"Of course not. It's on the way. Bye Mrs. Braun. I'll have her home by one." Ever the gentleman, Jesse would follow through on this promise; that would not be a concern. While Susan was grateful that she could go to bed without a worry when Kerry was out, she worried that her daughter was settling. Taking the easy way out.

Jesse opened the door to his new pearl-white F150 so Kerry could climb into the seat next to him. Once saddled in the truck he threw his arm around Kerry and gently kissed her on the lips. "I have a going away gift for you but I'm saving it for later," he teased.

Kerry drew her lower lip in and nibbled it. She leaned away from Jesse slightly as a familiar knot appeared in her stomach. She had been expecting Jesse to propose to her since Christmas. When he didn't propose at Christmas, Valentine's Day, her birthday in April or graduation, she thought she had skated through safely. Becoming a vet came before making any big commitment like marriage. Jesse would be a great husband. She just wasn't ready for the pressure.

"Sweet! Let's get this party started." She didn't want to appear ungrateful, but felt a little empty in her response.

Couples crowded the dance floor. "Shall we?" Jesse took Kerry's hands and soon they were boot-scooting the floor under the big tent. They knew this band and enjoyed the music. The Denim Rebels played at many of the events in the area. They were high energy and belted out popular country music, throwing in a few older tunes to keep the more mature crowd engaged. The female singer was a beacon to the cowboys in the crowd with her short leather hot pants, muscled legs, boots with bling, and leather vest. She tossed her hair as she threw herself across the stage, grinding to the beat of the bass guitar and drum. Cowboys flocked to her like moths to a flame. Jesse was not immune.

Jesse and Kerry had a great evening, dancing and hanging with their friends, promising to get together at Christmas when everyone would be back home from school or taking time away from their work to be with family.

Exhausted from long days of working at The Buffalo Diner, doing her chores around the ranch and packing for her big adventure, Kerry fell asleep with the sparkly tank top and makeup on, and jeans in a pile by her bed. Her alarm sounded at 4:30 the next morning. It wasn't until that moment that she realized Jesse had not given her the present he promised. "Phew! I dodged that one again," she thought to herself, feeling slightly embarrassed at her lack of gratitude.

She slipped her jeans back on. That was a distinct advantage she had over her friends who smoked. Her clothes were free of that offensive smell. She changed into a subtler t-shirt and headed toward the barn to see her horses, Gypsy, a Strawberry roan, and Prince, a handsome quarter horse and powerhouse who carried her through to many barrel racing wins. She would miss these two while away.

"My handsome Prince." Kerry curled her arm around the muzzle that breathed into her ear, getting as close as he could. Prince loved to snuggle, but only with her. She had thought about letting her cousin ride him since she was in the rodeo club and had a mediocre horse, but on the trial runs Prince would not respond to Sam. He only had eyes for Kerry. Gypsy stuck her head through the opening of her stall to greet Kerry. The first horse of her very own, Gypsy would always have a special place in Kerry's heart.

Gypsy was too spunky to be a reliable trail horse. She came to Kerry on her eighth birthday. "Every little girl needs a horse of her own, to ride in the fields and forget her troubles."

Kerry's dad loved her so much. Kerry never doubted that, even though there were times she felt like she hardly saw him. Ranching was hard for him. He didn't have the luck of his peers and most years he needed a second job to make ends meet. Her mom worked too. Theirs was not a charmed life, but there was never a doubt in Kerry's mind that they loved each other, and her, without fail.

And ride they did. Gypsy was Kerry's therapy for all disappointments, failures, and losses over the years. When her grandfather died from injuries suffered in a horrific farm accident, Kerry moved in with Gypsy for two weeks, emerging only for an occasional meal and to use the facilities. She changed her clothes once during the weeks they were together. They rode during the day, staying within sight of the house, or at least the road leading to the house, and sleeping in the barn at night. Kerry put up a cot next to Gypsy in the stall, and when she lay sobbing Gypsy nuzzled her to ease her sorrow.

Gypsy was special for many reasons. When friends came from town to visit, they rode Gypsy. She was well mannered with the kids. Kerry and her parents, on the rare day her dad had some time to kill, would ride the Badlands together, exploring the caves, digging in the hills for garnets and making up stories about how life was when the dinosaurs lived there.

Sometimes, Kerry wished she could enjoy those days again, when adulting was not looming over her and her parents were young.

She pulled a carrot from her pocket for Gypsy as she passed to get the tack. One last ride on Prince and she would be ready to drive across the state to start the next chapter. To the far end of the first pasture they rode, Kerry's free flowing hair trailing behind her, her slim, strong, thighs hugging the saddle. They rushed up to the barbed wire fence and halted.

Kerry lingered there, the reins loose in her lap as she watched the glorious sun rise over the landscape casting the pinnacles and buttes in a warm glow. Subtle shades of red, ochre, buff and lavender grey ombre emerged across the baby Badlands, the miniature version of the clay and rock monuments that planted themselves in the plains amongst the vast grasslands, a playground to squirrels and chipmunks.

She would miss the hills she spent her youth exploring, on foot, horseback and dirt bike. Mostly alone. Kerry's parents were not fortunate enough to have other children, so she was not only their daughter but also the son they never had. Her father didn't have a ready-made hand to help at the ranch, a sad reality to her. Kerry offered to stay and work for him instead of going to school but he would not have it. He knew of her aspirations and supported her completely, but Kerry knew that he paid a price for that support. Her father seemed to age faster than her friends' fathers. He had little time for fun and was always working. He never complained, and he always took her mom in his arms when he cleaned up after a day's work, telling her how much he loved her. Someday, Kerry thought, I will have this everlasting love too, one day.

CHAPTER 3

*W*ith the radio blaring, drowning out the cheap tires rolling on the hot pavement, Kerry made the trek across the state. Her excitement distorted time, so the trip was quicker than she thought it would be. A million things passed through her mind as she covered the nearly 300 miles. Her old Chevy Sonic was nothing special to look at but sure was reliable. It was a gift from her parents when she was sixteen. No big deal in their world, all the farm kids had cars. If they didn't, their parents would have to drive them to town for school and the many activities they had before and after school.

Kerry's dad taught her the basics of car care, like how to change the oil, replace a blown tire, and change out wiper blades. It was a crash course she went through before she could get the car. Yes, she was the son he never had. She didn't mind. Kerry enjoyed being independent and capable. She also found that guys respected her more when she shared mechanical knowledge with them.

She pulled onto the campus early mid-afternoon. There were upperclassmen wearing school colors with big carts helping the students unload their cars. Kerry was happy to have the help, although she was confident she could have managed herself. She opened the car doors and the trunk, and soon everything was on its way to her room. Kerry drove to the designated student parking, parked the car, and joined her belongings.

She took her mother's advice about getting organized and set herself up for success. She built a nest in and around her bed. Being an only child, Kerry never had a roommate before. Her mother bought and pre-washed some luxury cotton sheets in her favorite pink color. Putting them on her dorm mattress felt like claiming her new territory. She covered and fluffed two matching pillows in the same pink color. A boho-themed colorful comforter topped with some small, fun pillows with inspirational messages like 'today's the day' and 'you've got this' feathered the nest. Her childhood quilt, a gift from her late grandmother, hung safely in the closet for later use, if needed.

Kerry spent about an hour unpacking and organizing her belongings. She neatly folded new towels and washcloths and stored them on their designated shelf. Winter clothes were tucked in an under-bed storage container until needed, and other clothes were hung on the plush hangers her mother insisted she splurge on to personalize the closet.

As she expected to spend most of her time at the desk, Kerry took extra care to organize it well. She left behind the knick-knacks that decorated her childhood room and opted for a more minimalist desk with good lighting. She set up the phone-charging cube and placed her phone on the charger. With highlighters standing in penholders and sticky notes tucked neatly in the desk drawer, she gave the room a nod and found the college orientation materials.

Eager to be outside, she set aside a laundry basket of miscellaneous things to be put away later. She took the campus map from the folder and oriented herself. The campus was beautiful, with old trees and thick green, manicured grass, not like the wild sprawling grass of home. She walked around and familiarized herself with her classrooms. Securing a front-row seat brought some calm to Kerry, an anxious over-achiever. Her mother told her that professors noted those students who showed they were eager to learn.

As she walked around the campus with its stoic brick and limestone buildings, she nodded to the few other students she saw. Groups of upperclassmen dotted the campus as they fist-bumped, exchanged high-fives, hugged or otherwise greeted one another. It was comforting to see that friendships survived the summer break. She looked forward to making some of them herself. Only one other Buffalo Ridge student was attending Brookstone. He was not someone she would invite to a study group. He was a real party boy. But if she found herself in a bind, being from Buffalo Ridge, she was sure he would help her out, as she would him.

When she returned to her room, Kerry started organizing the last things left behind in the laundry basket. She spotted a pink package with a silver bow in the basket. She assumed it was something her mother had tucked in when she was packing the car. As she reached for the package, the phone on her desk sounded. She picked it up and noticed several missed messages.

Hi, honey. Just checking in to make sure you got there okay. Let us know. M&D. Her mother always signed her messages, even after Kerry explained to her, and showed her, that she had saved her number in her contacts and always knew when it was 'Mom' sending a message.

Hi M&D! Made *it here just fine and am moved in. Love u both! Will call you after dinner. Ker* She couldn't help herself. She added the Ker to keep with her mother's tradition.

She returned to the messages and saw one from Brandon. *Hey, beautiful. Thinking bout u. (wink emoji inserted).* Kerry didn't respond. She did not want to encourage the fool and hoped he would stay far away in Wyoming. She didn't need the intense distraction he could become. Tall, dark and handsome with too much time on his hands. Why on earth would she even have such thoughts? She loved Jesse.

The third message was from Jesse AKA 'Babe' in her contacts. *Hope u got my present. Forgot to give it to u. Slipped it in ur car. Luv u (heart emojis inserted).*

Kerry looked down at the package on the bed. "Well," she thought to herself. "It isn't a ring."

The door flew open and a petite dark-haired beauty walked in. She was a tiny package of bubbly carrying a laundry basket filled with clothes and hangers, followed by a male version of herself, and what was obviously their parents, each carrying a bundle they deposited on the empty dorm room bed. Kerry immediately recognized Gracie from her Facebook page.

"Hey, Ker! So great to meet you in real life!" Gracie grabbed Kerry and gave her a big hug against her tiny body. Kerry was average height but towered over this sweet girl. "This is my twin brother Gabe and our parents, Amy and Bill."

Without pausing for a response, Gracie moved right into giving everyone instructions.

"Mom, hang these up for me, please. Dad, there is another box in the car. Can you please bring it up? Hey Gabe, be a good brother and make my bed, will ya?" Gabe looked at her with disgust written all over his face. "It's ok, Ker will help you."

Kerry moved right into action, helping Gabe cover the bare mattress with hot pink sheets and a boho comforter. Since she did not have siblings, Kerry wondered if all brothers were as accommodating as Gabe was.

"Hey, it's nice to meet you, Kerry. Don't mind Gracie. She's not always so bossy, are you Grace?" Amy looked at Gracie with a 'you did it again' glance.

"Oh Ker, I'm sorry. I spent all summer, like the last four summers, teaching swimming lessons to a bunch of littles that, if they weren't always getting instructions, would have drowned one another, I swear. My apologies." Gracie smiled all the while she made her apology.

"Ah, that's ok. I'm a waitress. I'm used to taking orders." The group chuckled at this.

"Kerry, did you have your heart set on eating the slop in the cafeteria here? If not, we're going out for pizza. Would you like to join us?" Bill stood in the doorway holding the last box from the car. Kerry had only just met this fierce squad, but she already knew that she loved them. Hanging with them sounded like fun.

"I would love to join you! I think I will have plenty of opportunities to eat from the campus dining. Thanks!" She would open her package later. She tidied up her area and was ready to go with the Lambert family.

Her roommate came from Iowa City. She had a full-ride gymnastics scholarship and was studying nursing. Her dad was the manager of a big chain grocery store at home. Amy worked at the elementary school and Gabe was also college bound. He was staying in Iowa for school and had a baseball scholarship.

The evening with the Lamberts was a total blast. They laughed and told stories on one another. They learned all about Kerry, and freely passed around warm hugs.

"We're twins so we have to be close but he's a real butthead sometimes." Gracie gave Gabe a shoulder-to-shoulder bump as the family prepared to leave for home.

"We'll see who the butthead is when I finish my year on the dean's list and you barely squeak by." Gabe gave his sister a grin and pointed his finger her way.

"Bet you $50 I beat your GPA by the end of this school year," Gracie shot back.

"You're on." Gabe grabbed his sister in a bear hug. "Now, stay out of trouble and stick those landings."

"Yeah, yeah. See you guys in a few weeks." Gracie ushered her family out the door.

"Bye Lambert family. Nice to meet you all." Kerry enjoyed the evening. It was much more colorful than the evenings she had with her parents. The Lamberts were loud and funny.

"I'm going to shower tonight and hopefully avoid a mad rush in the morning. You need any help with anything?" Gracie looked over Kerry's side of the room. "Man, how did you get so organized so fast? You're one of those overachievers, aren't you?"

"Well, it looks like I'm in good company. I'm calling my folks and then wind down for the day if I can. I'm pretty excited about this whole college thing." Kerry's phone vibrated in her back pocket. She pulled it out and looked at it. "And, it looks like I have another call I need to make."

"Jesse?" Gracie knew about Jesse from Kerry's relationship status on Facebook: 'In a relationship with Jesse Davies'.

"Yep. See you in the morning if I'm sleeping by the time you get back here tonight." Thoughts about Jesse and a new life at school distracted her as she searched for pajamas.

CHAPTER 4

*T*he storm moved in suddenly from the east, bringing high winds and hail. Jesse ran to mount up. He saddled up his horse, Bandit. They raced to drive the cattle in to the shelter from the south pasture. His trusty dog, Buster, joined him and helped to keep those white-faced calves from wandering too far away. They were skittish with the change in weather. Every time a calf got out of line, its mother stopped in her tracks, waiting for it to catch up, slowing the whole process down. This was a job for two or three but his dad was taking the vehicles and equipment to the sheds as quickly as he and mother could manage it.

Chance was in Montana cowboying on the rodeo circuit and Steve was busy at his place doing the same thing; trying to beat Mother Nature. Some days this was a thankless job. Jesse got the cattle under the shelter as the dark skies swallowed the prairie and rained down golf-ball-sized hail. He, Bandit, and Buster all stayed under the shelter until the storm passed. It only took about 20 minutes, but during that time the fields took a beating.

Jesse spent the next few hours settling the cattle, surveying the damage and making a plan with his parents. He didn't realize his phone had died until he headed to bed. He plugged it into the charger but did not see until the next morning that he had a missed call from Kerry. She thanked him for the gift. Jesse couldn't tell if she liked it or not. Kerry didn't comment on any of the poems he had written for her. He was almost glad he had forgotten to give it to her in person, where she would have to feign excitement. Feeling stupid now, he stumbled to the breakfast table, his shoulders slumped as he drank his coffee.

"Hey cowboy, what's eating you?" His mother always seemed to know how he felt, even before he recognized it.

"Ah, nothing really. I missed a call from Kerry last night. Guess I'll talk to her in a few days." Jesse hadn't told his mother about the book of poetry and he wasn't about to spill his guts to her now. One disappointed woman in his life was enough.

"Gonna stick to that rule of no contact during the week, huh? I bet you can't do it. You two have been joined at the hip for years now." Yvette liked Kerry and wished her the best but wasn't sure she always brought out the best in Jesse. Sometimes his mood would be so dark. Not depressed but somewhat lost. "Thanks for your quick thinking yesterday in getting those cows in. There's nothing like a good storm to change your plans."

"Yeah, sure." Jesse was still lost in thought and berating himself silently. He never shared his writing with anyone and this was why.

Jesse spent the week putting up hay, working cattle and preparing for winter. Some fence needed repair after the wind ripped through. It seemed they could never mark 'done' on their list of things to do. One day, Jesse just hoped to declare "the end" to something. He needed that sense of closure sometimes instead of open-ended work hanging over him.

Jesse loved the ranch life. He did. But then, it's all he knew, and this ranch was the only one he knew, filled with clay and dried streams most of the year, snowstorms that blew in from nowhere to bury the place, and insidious hidden ice that took the footing right out from under you. Summer suns sucked the moisture out of every living thing leaving behind tinder ripe for ignition by the lightening reaching down from the dark thundering sky. Yes, he loved the drama nature displayed here. He also respected it.

By the time Sunday came around he was eager to hear from Kerry. They had agreed that she would start the call. He didn't want to bother her if she was studying. It was eight that evening, nine for Kerry, when his phone finally rang. She sounded distant. She and her roommate had been at the gym. Kerry was tired, exhausted from new demands and routine. She just wanted to say hi. The call was short and utilitarian, like it was being checked off her list.

"I promise I will call earlier next week. I miss you. Only eighty-two more days 'til I see you." And with that, Kerry was off to shower and read before bed. She was looking forward to the next week of school. He was happy for her but he was left feeling empty.

"This will be a long winter," he thought to himself. He opened his desk drawer, pulled out a handsome leather-bound journal he ordered online, and started writing. It was nearly two in the morning before he put his pen down. He wasn't sure what he was writing, but it felt good to be connecting with something. Pen to paper grounded him. It helped him see through his mind's clutter. Still missing Kerry but with a new calm inside, he slept.

This became the pattern. Kerry was settling into school and was very busy with her roommate and other new friends. She had little time to talk and looked forward to seeing him during the winter break. She still didn't mention his gift, which ended up being a relief for him. Jesse performed maintenance on all the farm vehicles during the winter so they were ready for the hard work of planting, plowing and harvesting come spring and summer. He hauled hay to the cows, chopped ice in the water tanks and plowed snow.

It had become an annual excursion for Jesse and his parents to travel to Vegas for a pro rodeo event. Chance was a roper and always made a good showing at the event. This made for a great break in November, away from the dark days and cold weather that hung around the Badlands.

This was brother Steve's first year alone on his ranch. His beautiful bride, Vikki, developed leukemia last year, and within two weeks of the diagnosis, was buried. Vikki was trained as an organic urban farmer. She brought to their marriage a business plan which included organic greenhouse gardening for an extended season, a new farmer's market and a community produce subscription service. Vikki was much loved in the community and in the few years of their marriage she crushed the first two goals for her business. They set a service for Perfect Pantry subscription boxes, which was scheduled to launch just weeks after Vikki died.

She was the picture of health. She went all out in pursuing her dreams but she was never pushy or over-the-top with her theories on a vegetarian lifestyle or living a chemical-free life. Even with the family, she was not pushy. Steve was so in love with Vikki that he let her manage her business and the house the way she believed was in their best interest. He continued to raise beef cattle and spray the crops for toxic weeds. When he wanted a steak, he grilled it and became a great grill chef who enjoyed throwing a big barbecue for the family and friends occasionally.

They were happy until that day when her annoying allergies became something much more ominous. Steve finally insisted that she go to the emergency room because she had such tightness in her chest she wasn't able to take a deep breath. She relented, and they drove the fifty-four miles to the nearest regional hospital. Vikki joked on the way, still not believing that there was anything profoundly wrong with her.

"We will look back on this next year and wish we had the money we'll spend to pay the hospital bill for having our new baby Davies." They had always wanted a family. They waited a year after their marriage before trying to get pregnant. Vikki stopped taking the pill, but three passed and they had not yet conceived. They didn't worry that they had not yet welcomed in little Davies.

The admitting nurse took her history in the emergency room. The emergency room doctor came to meet with them and examine her. Dr. Baldwin said that Vikki looked like maybe she had developed walking pneumonia but more tests were necessary. A CT scan of her chest showed bigger problems. They found multiple enlarged lymph glands. Then her blood tests came in. She was in full-blown acute myeloid leukemia and everything the doctors did to save her life failed. She opted not to embark on the chemotherapy journey, believing it would be futile in restoring her to the level of health and quality of life she desired.

Buffalo Ridge came together as a community and held prayer vigils, helped Steve on the ranch so he could spend time with Vikki at the hospital, and donated to the cost of her hospital care. Not because the Davies family needed it, but because watching out for one another is what communities do. Vikki was too sick to return home with hospice care. There were too few services available and no nurses in the area to hire. Rural living can be hard. She had a private room in the hospital for the days she was there.

"Steve, my knight in shining armor." On one of her last coherent days, before slipping into an unresponsive state, Vikki shared her heart with her husband. "You have been my everything. Together we have been so happy and I cannot thank you enough for all you have given me. I ask you for one last gift."

"What is that, my love? I will do anything for you." Steve lay beside his whisper of a wife, gently holding her.

"Find love again. You owe that to you. You owe that to me." He had no words to respond. He just lay, holding her, holding back his tears. Letting those heavy words pass through. He could not bear to think of someone else in his arms. He wanted only to keep her alive, any way he could.

Steve tried valiantly to keep her business dreams alive and manage the ranching operation. His dream was to open an experiential dude-ranch where city slickers could come get a taste of the good life. His dreams lay dormant after Vikki passed and only this year had he shown some renewed interest in seeing this project through. He elected to stay home from Vegas this year to work on that dream.

For Jesse, Vegas was a much-needed distraction from the falling grain prices in a precarious political time, extreme weather and the growing uncertainties about his relationship with Kerry. Kerry had been at school for only a few months but already they went two, even three weeks at a time with no call and only brief text message exchanges.

Hi babe, how are you? Jesse resorted to these generic inquiries.

Great. Running off to the library (or class, or the cafeteria, or the gym). *See you in December.* Kerry had little to offer but always held out the promise of connecting in December.

———

When December came, Jesse wasn't sure what to expect when Kerry got home. She spent the first day with her family. Jesse invited her to dinner. They had been friends for so long she was like one of the family to Jesse's parents, so they were eager to catch up with her. When she arrived, she gave Jesse a quick friendly hug and moved on to hug Yvette like they were long-lost best girlfriends. Kerry went to the kitchen to help Yvette with the final dinner preparations, leaving Jesse and his dad looking at one another and shrugging their shoulders as they moved to sit in recliners in the living room.

Yvette decorated the house beautifully, inside and out. Tall nutcrackers from Germany, an army of six, stood guard around the fireplace. There were three Christmas trees inside the house and one on the back deck. Each tree had its own theme. She decorated one in animals, another angels, and the third indoor tree held the family heirloom ornaments. Some were handmade by the children and they received others through the years as gifts from various relatives on vacation or while traveling.

"Son, maybe you would like to help me use up this Scotch." His father handed him a two-finger Scotch with a splash of water. Jesse recently turned twenty-one but for a few years had occasionally joined his father for a drink, particularly when contemplating something important.

"I believe I will. Thanks." Jesse took the glass and swallowed a big gulp of the burning amber liquid. It was enough to bring him back to reality. He was getting lost in his own unproductive, unflattering thoughts again.

Yvette and Kerry emerged from the kitchen, each carrying a large platter of food. "Dinner's on cowboys," Yvette blasted as she set the food on the table. Kerry locked eyes with Jesse. She noticed his sadness. She was feeling very much alive. They spent the evening catching up. Yvette and Dan shared Steve's progress with the organic gardens and his dude ranch, Chance's rodeo progress and Jesse's valiant efforts to save the livestock in the autumn storm. Jesse lingered on the fringes, nodding and throwing in an observation or two but he did not start any of the conversation and reverted to his reserved, unconfident self.

It embarrassed Jesse that his only bragging rights were from business as usual on the ranch. Jesse desperately wanted the attention off himself and onto something much more worthy. "So, tell us what it's like at the 'U' Kerry."

"It's so amazing being around such smart people." Immediately she knew this didn't come out right. "I mean, people who have studied different subjects for their livelihood, know things I could never dream of knowing, yet."

Jesse disappeared momentarily in thought. Did she know that he read and re-read poets like Frost, Whitman, and Poe? Did she ever read his book of poems created just for her? Suddenly Jesse felt a big chasm between him and Kerry and it wasn't just her being away at college. There was something bigger coming between them. He started to wonder if maybe there was someone else. He had heard rumors about some guy in Wyoming but never felt the strength to bring it up to Kerry. If it was true, then what? What did that say about him?

"I have learned more in one semester than I did in all four years under Mr. Keith," Kerry continued. Jesse looked at her quizzically. She was a top student. Was their education lacking or was college that complex?

"What is your favorite class?" Jesse hoped to make this an easy conversation for Kerry and move the evening along.

"Oh, it's definitely my anatomy class. In high school, we learned the basics, but this class is taking me deep into cell function, electrolytes, mitochondria, and ..." Kerry was very passionate about her experience in this class. Jesse found it somewhat overwhelming. "I'm sorry. I'm sure this is boring for you. It's just that I'm so happy to have this opportunity to delve deeply into the world I love so much." She paused briefly. "How was the trip to Vegas? Jesse said you had a good time."

"It was great to be away for a few days. Jesse got to celebrate his big birthday in style and Chance came away with a buckle." Yvette responded and for the first time realized Jesse and Kerry weren't as close as they used to be or she would already know these details.

"Big celebration, eh?" Kerry reached over and nudged Jesse with her fist. "That's the first I've heard about that."

"Eh, it was just a bunch of cowboys sitting around drinking beer. No biggie." Jesse didn't want to stir an already simmering pot. The guys made sure all the gals in the bar knew it was his birthday. He got birthday kisses from several of them. It was fun but he would have rather spent the time getting the attention from Kerry. Kerry was obsessed with her schooling. He didn't blame her for following her dream and being so very excited about it but he missed her affection. Kerry sent him a text to wish him a happy birthday.

Kerry did not invite Jesse to take her to Cathy and Jon's wedding. She had to be there early for hair and make-up. She told him she would meet him afterwards. Jesse drove separately but walked into the church with his parents. His breath caught when the processional of attendants started. Kerry was a stunning bridesmaid.

Cathy and Jon's wedding was beautiful, and it was great to see old friends home from college. A sense of nostalgia swept over Jesse and he had a hard time shaking it. He put on a smiling face around people, but as he wrote in his journal at night, he let it all out. He doubted the authenticity of everything in his life at that moment. Was he meant to be with Kerry? Was he a fool for not asking her to marry him; afraid he would interrupt her momentum with her dreams? Why was he so different from his siblings? They were dark, athletic, outgoing, and fun-loving. He was sandy-haired, fair-skinned, and serious in all things.

DAYS later the couple exchanged Christmas gifts. "Oh Jesse, it's so beautiful." It thrilled Kerry to see a beautiful bracelet in her Christmas gift and not a ring. She simply wasn't ready. She loved Jesse, but she also loved school and was excited to be living her dreams.

Jesse appreciated the sweater he got from Kerry. "Kerry, this is a beautiful sweater. Thank you so much. Will you wear it so it takes on your scent? Then I can snuggle it when I'm so lonely for you."

Kerry leaned in and whispered, "I already did." At a very basic, instinctual level Kerry and Jesse remained connected, even if life was interfering with their time together.

Kerry returned to school and dove into her classes at full steam. She took the opportunity to work as a lab assistant over the summer and didn't return to The Buffalo Diner. Her parents made several trips to visit her. Jesse drove down to the campus once. It didn't go well.

CHAPTER 5

*J*esse's phone buzzed as he pulled into the hotel parking lot. *Hey. Stuck in lab. B there in 30.*

Jesse stared at the text message. With lips tightened and shoulders slumped, he looked around. He drove across the state and Kerry couldn't make time for him. A sigh escaped as he slowly shook his head. He didn't know what he expected for the weekend but this was not a good start. They had barely spoken this semester, and he wondered if Kerry was avoiding him. And why?

K. Checking in hotel. Let me no when ur ready. He wasn't just going to sit around in the parking lot or on the steps of her dorm waiting for her. He could just as well be working cattle or fields. Rubbing his brow, he tried to rid himself of the building tension.

Abutting the stiffness of the asphalt parking lot was a beautiful green park with a walking path. He bypassed the hotel entrance and took the path. Walking through the beauty of a park near the hotel brought some temporary calm. He found a stone bench overlooking a flower and bush garden. Squirrels chased each other. Birds sang overhead, volleying shrill notes back and forth.

This lushness did not exist at his home on the plains, in the Badlands where the soil is dense clay and every year the winds carry off another layer and deposit it elsewhere. What else was he not seeing by staying on the ranch? More and more he had been wondering about this lately. He filled his writings with longings to be elsewhere, to explore questions and maybe find some answers.

About an hour later Kerry finally called. "Hey babe, sorry. I'm heading back to my room now. We had a mishap with an experiment and I had to clean it up. Meet you there in ten?"

Jesse was slow to respond. "Why don't you come over to the hotel?"

He threw his hand up in a silent rebellion to his unfolding feelings of defeat. "You know, there's a sweet park here and I can see a little bistro across the way."

He hesitated, unsure that he wanted to hang around. "We can get something to eat and you can get away from the campus for a while." Jesse needed to change things up. He didn't want to be in her territory to have the next conversation.

By the time Kerry arrived at the park Jesse was pretty worked up. He found it hard to make eye contact initially. His greeting hug was stiff and brief. They strolled to the sidewalk cafe and studied the menu in silence. After they ordered and got their drinks, Jesse suggested they take a break in their relationship.

"What does that mean Jesse? What kind of break are you talking about?" Kerry had changed into a cute sundress and put her hair in a messy topknot. She had matured over the first year of college. She was self-assured and excited about her studies. She was all consumed with her work-study job now and was taking classes throughout the summer. Jesse was not her priority now. Not even in the top ten priorities by his estimation.

"A clean break. Listen, Kerry, you're doing great here and following your dreams. I need to find mine. I am jealous of your singular focus on the goal. I don't have that and for me to be a good partner for anyone, including you, I need to go out and get that for myself." Jesse had not planned on this change. He thought he would spend some time hanging with his love but this felt right. He needed a break.

"Jesse. I'm sorry. I haven't been a very good girlfriend to you." Her eyes welled up as she reached out to him. Kerry never had confessed the kiss from Brandon to him. She loved school and not just the academics. She had made some good friends, and Kerry enjoyed spending time with them. It was new and fresh. He was familiar, comfortable, easy.

"Oh, but you have. You have been a model to me of setting your dreams and chasing them. I have taken too much for granted and have not pushed myself to create a life I want. I love you for that." Jesse was sincere and sad. Sad that it took parting for him to recognize and confess this to her.

Kerry went back to her dorm room, alone. Jesse drove back to the ranch instead of spending the night alone in a strange hotel bed without the promise of seeing Kerry the next day. The road trip did his head a lot of good. He made a plan that became more and more clear with each passing mile and he started to get excited. Stopping at a truck stop along the interstate, Jesse captured on paper the thoughts that were swimming through his mind before they disappeared. He ordered a chocolate shake and fries to ease his guilt for taking up space in the restaurant. He spent over an hour drawing up his initial plan.

Now, he would have to share it with his parents. He thought through the places he needed to go and the experiences he needed to have. His sister had been asking him for years to visit her in Arizona. If Steve agreed to help their dad with the ranch work over the winter, that would be a good time to escape the frigid winds and wet snow for the warmer high desert.

Hey butthead. Winter in AZ sounds good. Got room for me? Stella would get the text in the morning, he thought. He needed to test the waters to see how serious she was.

Within five minutes he had his answer. *Yahooooo! C U when snow flies!*

Stella outgrew Buffalo Ridge. She rarely came home. Like Kerry, she needed to prove herself. Jesse had the feeling that she was afraid if she returned home, the small town culture would trap her like a fly in a spider's web. Buffalo Ridge boys that she once dated, now men, longed for her to come home. They thought she would be the perfect cowboy's wife. Those men didn't know his sister. She was a cowboy. She was running cattle just like the men. No, better than. She was more intuitive than most men. She and her horse, Hedrick, were an incredible duo. They were poetry in motion when they were working cattle. Yes! This was his best next move.

JESSE RETURNED to the ranch just as the sun was rising. His adrenaline was rushing as plans were rolling in his head, which he then translated to the page. He was sitting at the kitchen table drinking coffee when his mom came in.

"Jess, I thought you were visiting Kerry this weekend. What's up?" Yvette was curious, but not entirely surprised. Her son was restless and preoccupied, even before he left for Brookstone. She would find him in the evening, after a full day of work, just staring off at the horizon, looking as if he had transported into another universe. He rarely went to town or hung with his old friends and often, when she got up in the night, she would see his bedroom light on.

"Well. I did. Then I left. Mom, Kerry has set awesome goals for herself and here I am like a fish flopping on the banks under the hot sun. Any original idea I had has dried up and I need an infusion of life. I'm trying to think through how I can get out and explore some. I have some ideas but need to draw a roadmap and talk to more people before I break it to dad."

"You know we love you, Jess. Your dad will support you." Sylvia moved her hand from the warm coffee cup and placed it on his shoulder, a showing of solidarity. Though a grown man, this son was her most fragile.

"Yes, I know mom. I just don't want to dump and run, leaving him without help. I'm going to see if I can go find Steve and chat with him." Jesse knew his parents were supportive. They would be excited for him to explore the world some. They would love for him to remain in the area long term.

"You know you'll find him over in the greenhouse, keeping Vikki's dream alive. That man is the most faithful husband." Yvette admired Steve for his resolve but also realized his commitment to Vikki's ghost paralyzed him.

"Of course. I'll be back in time to help Dad with the spraying." Jess took the last swig from his coffee and put the empty cup in the dishwasher, gave his mother a quick squeeze and launched out the door.

Steve was right where his mother said he would be. He was tending to the young plants growing in the raised beds in the greenhouse. He loved these plants as much as Vikki did and she had taught him well. He consulted the three-ring binder that contained her multiple instructive checklists. Vikki's organizational skills were unmatched, and she was a visionary in business. She attached sticky notes to binders with her ideas: 'recyclable boxes', 'discount for box reuse', 'distribution points - hardware store, farmer's market, rodeo grounds'.

"Hey man, good to see you!" Steve looked up from his work when Jesse walked in. "Thought you were off to see the girlfriend."

"Yeah, about that. It's not working." Jesse hung his head. He was in the company of a great romantic who had manifested the perfect wife, something Jesse wasn't sure would ever happen for him.

"Didn't see that coming. You okay?" Steve had gone to college. That's where he met Vikki. She was the only woman he had fallen in love with. He had girlfriends before, but Vikki sparked something that even he didn't know was lying dormant within him. He wanted that for his baby brother, whether he found it with Kerry, or elsewhere.

"Yeah, man, I'm good. I was feeling like we weren't on the same page. You know she's got big dreams and so far, I've just kept my lazy ass here at the ranch. I haven't developed any bigger picture for myself. I didn't realize until recently just how much of a rut I was stuck in." Jesse was trying to convince himself, as much as Steve, that he believed there was something bigger out there for him.

"So, that's why I'm here. I need you to help me out." That caught Steve's attention. Jesse explained to Steve how he would go to Arizona over the winter and spend some time with Stella but he didn't want to leave his dad high and dry without enough help.

"Sure, I'm around anyway. The greenhouses are closed up, except for the poinsettias around Christmas. By spring though, I'm planning to be pretty busy with the dude ranch. I'm meeting with a website designer next week to get the site up and do some advertising." Steve was following his dreams, and it felt great.

"Wow! I'm so happy to hear you are getting closer to getting that thing off the ground. You and Vikki shelled in those bunkhouses and mess hall. When are you going to finish those out?" Jesse worried that he was taking his brother off course.

Steve consulted his checklist again and measured out organic fertilizer according to Vikki's instructions. "This really cool thing happened. Everything is just coming together. So, I was talking to Mr. Roberts, you remember, the vo-tech teacher? He said this would be an awesome opportunity for his students to get some real-life experience in plumbing and wiring. I just have to provide the materials and those guys and gals will come out here. Commercial level inspections will be done so the insurance company doesn't throw a fit." Things always worked out for Steve. Except for Vikki. That was one part of the dream that was now forever shadowed, or so it seemed.

"You got a name for this place yet?" Jesse would like to spread the word when the time came and hoped that Steve had a catchy name.

"Well, that's where it gets a little tricky because part of the attraction will be for organic gardening. I haven't come up with a name that marries dude and garden but I'm working on it." Steve had long lists of rejected names on his legal pad. Nothing seemed to flow.

"How about a contest? That would be a great way to get more ideas. If there is one you choose, the winner could get a free vacation at the garden and dude ranch." Jesse had been exploring writing contests for himself and thought the idea might just work here.

"Dude, I'm gonna miss you! That's why you're the geek in the family. You have all these brainy ideas." Steve admired his brother's brilliance, even if he could out muscle Jesse without even trying.

"I'll only be a text away. You do know how to use text, right?" Jesse was kidding his brother who had sent some hilarious text messages, the byproduct of fat fingers and autocorrect. "Anyway, I'm not going for a few months. I will catch Dad and break it to him."

"He'll cry like a baby. You're his gopher, you know. Go-for this and go-for that." Steve measured Jesse's response. Sometimes, he thought, I may not give this kid enough credit. "Naw, he's gonna take it okay but he'll take a bet on you returning after your walk-about and the odds will be in his favor."

"Could be. Catch ya later." Jesse slid into his truck and headed down the gravel road to home. Home, for now. The two ranches were only five miles apart. Jesse felt his world closing in on him and it didn't feel good.

CHAPTER 6

$\mathcal{B}$y the end of the second year of living in Brookstone University's dorms, Kerry was ready to move off campus. She continued to work in the biology department lab and had volunteered at a local vet clinic to get some practical experience. Academically, she was soaring. Her professors took a shine to her and saw to it she had insider opportunities to meet guest lecturers, travel to conferences and take part in relevant research projects. Kerry was all business at school, with the professors. She had little time for a social life but did go out occasionally.

"Hey Ker, do you ever talk to that old boyfriend of yours? Jesse?" Gracie was getting ready to move off campus too. The two of them had become close friends, and they supported each other in their endeavors. Gracie was a gymnastic superstar in the collegiate circuit. She barely had time for schoolwork. Kerry helped her, when she could, to bone up for exams and get through projects but Gracie was bright, too, and did well. She and Gabe both did well, and both made the Dean's list every semester, as did Kerry.

"You know, it's funny you should bring him up. When I went home for Christmas I had hoped to see him but it seems he has moved to Arizona with his sister." Kerry didn't know Stella well. She was older and had left Buffalo Ridge before Kerry started dating Jesse. "But, I came across his book when I was packing up."

"What book is that?" Kerry had not shared Jesse's writing with Gracie.

"Well, when I first came to school, in fact, the day you moved in, I found a present from him. Looking back now it's kind of funny. Before I left for school, we went out and he told me he had a present for me. I tried to keep him distracted all night because I was afraid that present would be a promise ring or something."

"Oh my God! That's how it is in small towns, isn't it? Catch that girl before she flies the coop." Gracie often teased Kerry about her less-than-worldly life experience. Such a goody-two-shoes.

"Ha! Yeah, it is for some. But anyway, I found this present when I unpacked my car. When I opened it I found this book. It's all hand-written stories and poems by Jesse." Kerry caressed the blue leather cover of the book with her open hand.

"Really? Did you know he was a writer?"

"No, that's the thing. We never talked about it. I only read a few pieces and it kind of freaked me out. He filled the pages with feelings and emotions and really beautiful stuff. I thought he was maybe trying to tell me something in those words. I was afraid of what it was so I just put it away." Kerry only now realized how unkind it was not to read Jesse's work and even more so, not to talk to him about it.

"What did you say to him? Hey, your stuff is good but I ain't like that?" Gracie giggled.

"I didn't say anything. What could I say? I barely looked under the cover and now, I feel so bad. I'm going to read these stories. Then I'll see how I feel about telling Jesse. Now, I feel so mean but nobody has ever poured their heart out to me like that before. I just didn't know what to do."

"Girl, you need therapy. That boy liked you! Anyway, now you need a little different therapy. We are out of school for the summer and it's time for us to play a little." Gracie's idea of play was to go rollerblading or hiking. Kerry would rather volunteer at the animal shelter.

"Okay but we can't be out too late, we both work tomorrow." They both had two jobs for the summer and Gracie still had training during the week. Kerry set the book atop the bedding in her laundry basket and picked it up. She looked around at the lifeless walls that once boasted their favorite memes and selfies. The bookshelves were erased of their knowledge and the beds were bare and cold.

"Always the one to rain on my parade, aren't you? Let's take the last of these things to the car, say goodbye to this dump and head to OUR place. Tell me you're excited." Gracie hooked a half-dozen hangers to dangle from her wrist and grabbed the last box off her desk. The two headed to Kerry's car leaving behind their youth. They had their own place now. Life was starting anew for the girls, both now out of their teens and ready to adult.

Kerry lay in her new-to-her bed that night and re-read the first pages of Jesse's book. As she read, her inner voice narrated her thoughts. "He was trying to tell me something. He was trying to tell me about the intricate interconnectedness of nature, the brutality and harshness of the weather, and the sweetness of a gentle kiss under the stars. Boy, did I miss it. I was so excited to be away from that place and spread my wings, I just didn't see it." A tear slid down her cheek as she remembered the closeness they once shared. A kinship built from sharing the same stomping grounds, the same community and once, the same dream. Did she still want to return to Buffalo Ridge and start a veterinary practice? She wasn't sure anymore and, who would be there to help her now that Jesse had moved on?

THE SUMMER FLEW by with her jobs and school. Dreaming about her future practice motivated Kerry to put in the long study hours. Every vision was grounded in Buffalo Ridge. She made it a point to look at a half-dozen area vet clinics, to get a feel for different practices. She met with clinic owners or managers, toured the facilities, found examples of business models and allowed herself to contemplate the options. Nothing moved her vision beyond Buffalo Ridge where she saw herself being a generalist available for livestock and household mammals. She didn't favor reptiles and would refer them to the specialists outside her clinic.

Her mom drove down and took her shopping, cleaned up the apartment and treated the girls out to dinner over the July fourth holiday. It was a welcome interruption to their usual routine, and it was always great to spend time with Mom. She shared her exploration of options with her mom, who seemed surprisingly relieved that Kerry could make a home in Buffalo Ridge. This seemed a change of heart from her mom but she didn't want to pry. In time, everything would work out, as it needed to.

Because she attended school year-round and took heavy loads, Kerry was an advanced student and would graduate ahead of the class she began with. She had to take her graduate school entry exam and start preparing applications for veterinary school. She would then be faced with another big decision. Where would she go for graduate school?

Gracie already had plans to go to Nebraska for her graduate program. They had grown so close that Kerry considered following her but the school did not have the exact program that Kerry wanted.

CHAPTER 7

"Come on cowboy, grab your bedroll." Stella kicked her boot against Jesse's bare foot hanging off the couch. "Dang boy, when did your feet get so big?"

The October chill was in the early morning air.

"Brr. I thought Arizona would be hot. You need to turn the heat up." Jesse drove in late the evening before. He turned his trip out from Buffalo Ridge into a mini-vacation. He explored Estes Park, Colorado in the Rocky Mountains. The natural beauty of the area with fall foliage and wild animals, including moose and elk, moved him. He enjoyed the serenade of the elk bugle during mating season. The vast wildness and sheer beauty of the rugged mountains blanketed in white resided in his memory.

Jesse didn't realize how much he would appreciate those few days off to transition between working for his father and working with his sister, which he also thought would be like a vacation. Boy, was he wrong.

"Come on, sissy boy. These cattle aren't going to wait all day. I've got a horse for you. Bring your dry socks and clean underwear." They hadn't talked about what Jesse would do while working for his sister. He just knew he needed a change of scenery and she was eager to have him.

"You see that orange sky over there? That's the national forest land where our cows are pastured. That blazing hot orange is a raging wildfire heading right for them. We need to push these cattle back and across the river. It's about a thirty-mile drive then we'll be on horseback. You do still ride a horse, right?"

"Girl, you know I can and I can throw a rope too. Who else you got coming?" The countryside, which was far different from what Jesse had imagined, intrigued him. He never thought to research it and prepare himself. He imagined an environment more like the Vegas area, not high country desert with canyons, craggy walls and a mix of trees and cacti. The fabric of this landscape was heavily textured and uninviting. Many parts appeared uninhabitable for man and beast. It made for great writing material though.

"Gus will be coming along. You've got nothing on him. He'll have those cattle marching a straight line right down those hills in no time."

Jesse guessed that Stella got up with the moon still high in the night sky to get everything ready. She loaded the horses in the trailer with all their tack and some feed and the dog was sitting in the cargo bed when Jesse climbed into the old truck. Stella had no need for a shiny new truck when the old one worked just fine. She would much rather be riding atop a horse, anyway. She felt no need to apologize for the layers of dried mud and dust smeared across the floor and dirty paw prints embellishing the seat. Stella slammed her door closed and started the truck up. She put the shifter in drive and started to take off.

"Wait, isn't Gus coming with us?" Jesse didn't see any other buildings around where they would stop to pick someone up and he wasn't in the bunkroom of the little shelter they stopped in.

"He's back there." Stella motioned to the cargo bed.

"Ha! That mutt's your hand? Bet you're glad I came by, aren't you?" Jesse knew his sister was tough, but this was ridiculous.

"You don't always work alone, do you?" Now he was getting worried about her mental health.

"Well, I had a fella helping me but we didn't see eye to eye about my jeans so I ran him off." Stella was a beautiful woman with long dark hair and tanned face. Her physique showed the hard work she did every day. She was strong and Jesse admired that. In so many ways she was becoming a role model for him.

"Um, he didn't like your jeans?" Jesse wasn't sure where this was going. Fearing he might intrude on her personal space, he hesitated to ask for clarification. Jesse also assumed Stella cherished the silence on these trail rides of hers. He wasn't there to bend her habits.

"He liked 'em just fine, but only when they were not covering my body. I sent his grabby hands to New Mexico to a buddy down there. He'll make sure he leaves my jeans alone." Stella likes her solitary life. Well, not completely solitary. She had her cows. Her scrappy friends living off the spotty greens of the high desert.

"Geez Stella. You probably shouldn't be out here alone." Jesse wondered how she managed out here alone. There must be coyotes and wolves, and apparently men with a fetish for jeans, or is that a non-jeans fetish? Anyway, what if her horse came up lame?

"I'm not alone. You're here. Now, drink your coffee. I hope you like it black. I don't carry the Frou Frou stuff to put in it. There's a breakfast burrito in that bag there for you too. I'm about ready for my second breakfast. Hand me one too, will ya?" Stella handed him a thermos and pointed to the bag. When she got her burrito, she ripped off a piece and fed it to Gus through the back window.

"Here you go, boy. Warm your blood up so we are ready to

move those cows when we get there." Gus grabbed the snack with gusto and gulped it down. He kept watch over them as they moved through the dry grass and hills.

"This is a lot different from what I thought it would be." Jesse noticed the trees amongst the huge boulders. Much like the Badlands of home, parts of the high desert appear to be a forgotten land of long ago with untamed stone structures whittled by water and ice from long ago. Snow had fallen and melted everywhere but the tops of the highest peaks. There were still carpets of green grass where the moisture from the melted snow stood. On the journey, Stella pointed out small cliffs and clefts where, with adequate rain and snowfall, small waterfalls flowed.

"I bet you were expecting sand and cactus, weren't you? Well, here in the high desert we have seasons. Not as dramatic as those you have in South Dakota but we get snow in the winter. Unfortunately, in the past year we have had too little snow and rain so we are a tinderbox here." Stella pointed out the dry creek beds and patches of dry grass that usually were plenty green. She explained how she had to move the cattle more frequently now because the land wouldn't sustain them for longer periods. Charred marks scuffed the ground and splintered trees where lightening reached out of the sky and scorched the earth and its ornaments.

"Global warming at its finest, I guess." Jesse wasn't exactly sure where he stood on the Global warming debate. Being a cattle rancher and one of the supposed culprits put him in a precarious position. One thing he knew for sure; the weather patterns were changing, even in his relatively short lifetime, and to hear his parents' stories, it has transformed in theirs.

"Yeah, not sure how much longer my boss will take these risks. When these cattle can't graze on the federal land anymore, he's done." Stella seemed to know a lot about this business.

"Why's that?" Jesse's family owned their land outright,

having passed it from generation to generation, with the taking generation growing the land mass when possible. He was not familiar with the federal lease program. She explained how the ranch helped the federal lands by regularly grazing. The fire was not on grazed land. It was on land that was not being used. It was close enough to dry trees that it could hop its way to where they were now, consuming the fuel used for the cattle along the way.

"It's like if the buffalo in the Badlands were under private ownership but the national park still wanted them to graze there. They would charge the livestock owner a nominal fee and require them to follow a grazing rotation to protect the national grasslands. The owner would have to maintain the fencing and carry liability insurance in case one of those burly creatures stepped in front of a tourist's car and smashed it." Stella had not forgotten where she came from: a beautiful bluff overlooking the colorful formations of the Badlands that tourists came far and wide to see in the summer.

"Gotcha. How many cattle are there?" The land before them was so vast that he expected Stella to say a thousand head or more.

"There's 300 head somewhere out there in about 4,500 acres of land. We've got it sectioned off into five pastures and we move them around depending on how the grazing land is holding up. We work hard not to overgraze any pasture." Stella seemed to be a master with what she was doing.

"I can't believe this!" Stella said as a shiny red Cadillac Escalade approached them on the road. "That fool!" Seeing this displaced vehicle in pristine condition, without even a gravel nick in the windshield, caused Stella to become slightly apoplectic Jesse noticed. She looked in her rearview mirror and under her breath told Gus to take a seat. He had already started barking at the other vehicle. She stomped on the clutch and downshifted, causing the truck to whine and slow abruptly.

"Brandon Cage, as I live and breathe, out here getting

dusty with the hired hands." Stella shouted out her mostly open window to the man in the Escalade.

"Nice to see you Stella. Looks like the fire's gonna cause some damage up there. Hope you got all your cattle in." Brandon didn't take his blue eyes off Stella and she glared right back at him. She would not let this city slicker push her buttons. Not today. She had work to do and cattle to rescue.

"We've got it under control. Don't you worry your pretty little head about it. Now get yourself back to the city where the rest of the suits live. Let us manage our herd." Stella started rolling her window up.

"I could sure use that spicy attitude of yours on my board Ms. Stella. You sure you don't want to come work for me?" Brandon Cage had not stopped smiling since pulling up. Clearly there was some history here that Stella had not shared with Jesse. The tension between the two was nearly visible in a belted cloud that encircled their torsos.

"I have no interest in schmoozing with the likes of you, Mr. Cage, and your special interest groups who want to destroy this land. Get on out with you now." Stella showed a real dislike for this guy. Real, or feigned, Jesse couldn't tell.

As the vehicles parted ways, Jesse started to ask his sister for an explanation. All he got was, "That Brandon Cage is a snake and you need to stay far away from him." Jesse sensed there was more to the tension between the two of them but he let the matter drop. He had just arrived. It was too soon to pry.

They crossed the last cattle guard into the national forest land, went a few miles deeper into the forest and came upon a clearing. A two-sided, roofed open shed stood on a patch of worn dirt enclosed in a sorting pen. The cattle motel, Stella called it.

A small building sat nestled in the juniper trees and sagebrush. Stella explained that this was the tack house and bunkroom. "Nothing fancy but it almost keeps the rain off ya."

Jesse pulled a half-dozen five-gallon buckets of supplies

from the truck and hauled them to storage. Talking sweetly to them and patting them gently, Stella untied the halter ropes and lovingly backed the horses out of the trailer. These beautiful horses were more than her work partners; they were her trusted confidants. Reassuring them and managing their comfort, she saddled and outfitted the horses for their days on the trail. Supplies were tucked in the well-worn tooled leather saddlebags. A coiled rope was hung on each saddle horn.

Stella threw a pair of leather chaps to Jesse. His brows furrowed, a question forming in his mind. Anticipating the explanation, she told him that many trees and bushes on the trail were thorny. The chaps, which he rarely wore on the plains, would protect him. She had also insisted he wear a long-sleeved shirt, a hat and bandana.

With the truck secured next to the tack house, they mounted their rides. The horses were tall and sturdy. They easily managed the loads they carried. Stella guided them to an opening in the sage. A livestock trail, hidden amongst the brush, came into view as they approached. The horses moved with precision and confidence on this familiar trail.

"This is like no other riding you have done." Stella warned him. "The land is very rocky and we will move slowly and uphill. I actually moved most of the cows last week so we will collect the stragglers on this ride."

"How long will we be out here? That's a lot of land." Jesse didn't have a bedroll or a tarp for a shelter or anything with him if they would be out here overnight.

"I imagine it will take two, three days. What's the matter, you have a date I don't know about?" Stella shot back.

"Ha! What do you know about dates hiding out here in no-man's-land? I think you just insulted your last prospect down there on the road."

"Brandon Cage is a competitor. He wants this land for his own demonic reasons and I'm here to see that he doesn't get it." Stella was adamant about her position and her disdain for the city slicker was obvious.

With that they fell into silence and started up the trail. They rode through dense, dry brush, ambling uphill for about an hour and a half before they crested a hill and Jesse got a view of the canyon below. It was rugged with granite boulders and a more rigid and sturdy version of the spires seen in the Badlands. Juniper forests dotted the sloping hills forming the canyon walls.

"You have cattle out there?" Jesse motioned toward the millions of acres of land that comprised the basin they rode in. He was in disbelief that the unlikely, inhospitable rangeland before them could sustain a herd of cattle.

"That's right. Like I said, these are just the stragglers. According to my count, there are twenty-one of them out there now. Gus will scare 'em out of the crevices and brush and get them headed in the right direction. We have a couple more hours to go though, before we start seeing them. They rode in silence for nearly an hour. The horses were sure-footed and instinctively knew where to go.

Jesse found himself lost in thought. His horse, Rowdy, did all the work. The slow and steady stride lulled Jesse, and he had flashes of rides shared with Kerry. In a time that seemed long ago and a place far away they rode the Badlands' hills and plains. Unlike here, their horses were free to open the throttle and run in the open grasslands. At the end of the ride, they dismounted and embraced. Jesse looked down into Kerry's eyes, dancing with excitement. He found her mouth with his and they kissed there, amongst the wild grass, in the open plains. The rare tree may give them shade. They walked hand-in-hand across the crusted clay floor while their horses cooled down.

Jesse's horse stopped as the foursome, horses and riders, came upon a fallen tree blocking the trail. Jesse was jarred back to the present. He looked around and registered the reason for the abrupt stop. Jesse was in awe of the contrasting terrain, the colors, the singing birds and his sister's natural fit into this wilderness. "This is really amazing country. So wild and rugged."

"I know. I love it. Twelve years I've been working up here and not one day have I regretted it. Well, maybe that day I was staring down a rattler sitting at the foot of my bedroll." Stella's eyes grew. She sat up stiffly and clutched her shirt, as if she could still see the rattler at her feet now.

"Seriously? I would have freaked out I think. We have rattlers but I sleep in a bed, off the floor, in a house, and they don't come in." Jesse shook his head as he imagined his sister staring down that snake and thinking how frightened he would be. Damn, she's brave, he thought.

"This is all my bedroom. I have three camps set up out there." Stella wove her hand across the horizon.

"I was wondering why we were traveling so light if this would take some time. Guess I have a lot to learn about this land of yours." Jesse was in awe of the life Stella was leading. She was a real cowboy, living close to the land, playing hide-and-seek with coyotes and holding standoffs with rattlers.

CHAPTER 8

*F*or two days the pair scrubbed the brush and rounded up the stray cattle. Smoke blew in and the sky glowed a brilliant orange at night. During the day a dark cloud of dust and ash hung over the canyon. They stopped frequently to rinse the bandanas they used over their mouths to filter the air. Some places were worse than others. They rode through pockets where a cloud of smoke clung to the crevices and other areas, and other areas where the breeze pushed the air around so they barely notice the dense air.

These cattle were not like any Jesse had ever seen before. Gentle, slow, lower to the ground and smaller than the herds he was used to wrangling. Stella explained how the cows were specially bred to manage this vegetation and the terrain. She shared the history of Barzona Angus and Brangus bulls and how breeding over several generations improved the cattle's ability to thrive in this difficult environment. Jesse wondered if Kerry was familiar with the breed and what she would think of this country. He may have ended their dating life but he couldn't stop thinking about her.

Jesse and Stella walked their horses about as much as they rode, dismounting to reach the highest and lowest places in the canyon. Gus, a blue heeler Labrador rescue dog, occasionally got distracted flushing quail from the shrubs, but overall he was a terrific herder.

THE SECOND NIGHT, as the sun started to reflect pink on the canyon walls, they rode up on one of the ranch's campsites. There was a wall tent and some gear sheds. Stella went to work putting together some dinner. Jesse unsaddled the horses and settled them for the night. After dinner they sat around the campfire, reflecting on the rugged beauty surrounding them. Stella pointed out various ridgelines on the horizon and shared some history of this ranching operation and how she came to be the foreman.

At one point she reached out to pet Gus, stretched out next to the fire. "One of the hands I worked with was kinda sweet on me."

Stella told many colorful stories from her years on the ranch. She started to explain and suddenly busted out with a poem:

> *"A cowboy came a callin'*
> *on the eve of Christmas Day.*
> *Said he was a haulin'*
> *just to pass the time away.*
>
> *He stayed a spell to work the trail*
> *and watch the sun set pink.*
> *In the end his breath was stale*
> *from all the snus and drink."*

Jesse leaned in; a big grin grew across his face as she continued.

"Atop the cold stone boulder
the cowboy held a present.
A sack slung from his shoulder
the size of a pheasant.

John Marshall was a simple man
he didn't care for fuss.
Before he saddled up his van
he gifted me with Gus."

"Woah, I didn't know you wrote poetry!" A warm feeling spread through him as he realized he had witnessed yet another of his sister's talents. She was coloring with his crayons. Curious now, he hoped she would share more.

"Ha! That's lame but I have a lot of time on my hands out here. Sitting alone around the fire, keeping company with cattle and squirrels, I sometimes get a little ditty playing in my head. I have about a dozen notebooks with crazy things in them, like this one." Stella pulled a tattered notepad from the inside pocket of her Carhartt jacket and waved it toward him.

"I write a little too but it's nothing as structured as that. Just a bunch of musings on paper." Jesse thought back to the book he shared with Kerry and wondered what had ever happened to it. Someday maybe he would have the nerve to ask her if she ever read it.

The sweet smell of Italian sausage and rice stuffed green peppers filled the air as Stella pulled the Dutch oven from the fire grate. Steam clouds flew as she lifted the heavy cast iron lid. She had become a competent camp chef and was thrilled to have Jesse to cook for. When she traveled alone, she often ate gorp or raw food. Stocking her freezer with trail foods she could pack out and heat had, for her, become culinary art. Out here under the stars in the cool air, it felt good to get something warm in the belly to sleep on. Trail mix and jerky were fine for lunch but didn't help them get a good night's sleep.

The dishes were done. Stars danced overhead in the dark sky, preserved from city lights. Thoughts, rhymes and stories were penned in her notebook. She thumbed through the small book. Pages topped by a wire coil; shreds of paper evident from discarded pages. As she thumbed through the pages, her face alternated between smiling, rolling of the eyes, and a gentle shaking of the head; she marked a handful of pages.

Stella penned satires of stories she heard, captured images from places she visited, and painted humorous images of people and events. She told of some colorful characters she had shared the trail with and some mystical, magical places she captured in her gritty, grounded way. Jesse was captivated. Her words amused and entertained him. He found his toe tapping the meter of the lines as she read them. A portion of his brain made an unseen list of rhyming words. His creative mind envisioned the wise but unfortunate cowboys she spoke of, the wild horse in the canyon and the thundering sky. He was filled with pride and was grateful to be with a kindred spirit.

"Tell you what. There's a cowboy poet's gathering coming up. Let's go get us some culture." The two chuckled and made a plan.

BY THE TIME Friday evening rolled around, they were safely back in town and the cattle roundup was a success. All twenty-one head were safely relocated away from the fire. They would restock supplies, wash the soot from their hair, and take some time to play. Stella kept a watchful eye on the sky and an ear to the network of communication about the fire. Silent prayers for rain infused the night air as they lay in reflection before sleep.

Smoke rolled in from the wildfire consuming vast areas in difficult terrain. On windy days, the smoke blew into town and stirred up the community. They had no understanding of fire science but were quick to criticize the professional fire management team. There was a lot of talk wherever they stopped while running errands. They did their best to relay accurate information they heard while meeting with the fire management headquarters.

"Fear. Now that's something to write about. It takes our brain cells and common sense and turns them into mush." Jesse was keen to observe human emotion and reflect it in his writing. He turned it on himself too and explored his own fears. The theme of not being good enough, so prevalent in his past, seemed to be less prominent now. Maybe, he thought, he was growing up.

In the time since he and Kerry were no longer together, he had taken a few women out. He had no intention of getting serious, so when he found they were texting or calling frequently he broke it off, explaining that it was him, not them, and he just wasn't ready for a serious relationship. He also never was comfortable with anyone the way he was with Kerry, and he wasn't sure that would ever change.

The Cowboy Poet's round-up venue was the local community college. The parking lot was filled with dusty pickup trucks, some pulling trailers. Ladies in denim skirts and men in cowboy hats filed into the auditorium, greeting friends and neighbors as they passed. Stella stood out in the crowd with her thick, raven black hair hanging loose, tight jeans tucked in her dressy boots, and a broad smile. It seemed everyone knew his sister.

"Hey Stella, need any help to get those cows out of the danger zone?" Cowboy after cowboy offered to help her save the cattle. And they weren't just the single men; these cowboys were all ages, sizes and marital status. They were a cowboy community and Stella was a respected member.

"Thanks Harv. My brother Jess here and I are doing okay."

Stella introduced Jess to the locals. He shook hands with the men and boys and tipped his hat to the women and girls. This culture, the cowboy culture, clung fast to such traditions and Jess felt good being part of it. The genteel culture suited him. His peers rarely showed the same respect for one another and their elders. And so the evening went on with Jesse meeting Stella's friends and neighbors, swapping stories of fires past and hopes of rain.

The ranch that Stella worked for was a sponsor of the gathering. Stella had the honor of saying a few words on behalf of the ranch as part of the evening's welcome and introductions. She garnered rousing applause.

The first presenter was an old-time singer and songwriter by the name of Howie LaDuke. Mr. LaDuke had homesteaded in the area some fifty years prior. He took up the guitar to keep himself occupied on the trail in his early days. His songs were about life on the trail and dreams of pretty girls back home. He started his performance by apologizing to his wife of forty years. The other women he was singing about meant nothing. The crowd laughed. He shared gratitude for having his wife by his side as they overcame drought, floods, and a child's death. Now they celebrate a large family and happy cows. Jesse got a kick out of his lyrics. He sang lines like, *Oh pretty Sadie back in the city, you'll thank me for leaving you there where the spiders and bats stay out of your hair.* Mr. LaDuke was well respected by the crowd, not so much for his talent as for his long-standing contribution to the cowboy lifestyle. Some liked the music. All laughed.

Poets of all ages shared their favorites or tested new works out on the audience. Jesse did not know this was an industry. Artists stood behind tables lining the lobby. They sold CDs, books, and postcards. Media artists had prints for sale and sculptors displayed their work, which were for sale but not within the price range of most.

Jesse found himself drawn to a book of poetry with a brilliantly colored cover. The artist filled the page with vibrant hues like those seen in the dramatic Arizona sky, more colorful than usual with the fire providing a magnificent backdrop. Jesse chatted with the author about the book as he bought a copy.

He hadn't read any strictly cowboy poetry and looked forward to studying the style. Jesse stood across the table from the author with one long blue-jean covered leg cocked slightly to the side so he could lower his tall lanky body. He listened intently to the things that inspired the artist and then commented on the beautiful cover. The poet grinned and nodded toward a young woman standing behind a table across the lobby.

"That's my niece, Kendra. She's the artist. Kendra would love to hear you rave about her cover. She's new at this and none too sure she's on the right track, like we all are." The cowboy poet had a lot of years in the saddle and his poetry filled a book so he must have invested a lot of seasons at that craft.

"Thank you, sir. I hope to see you again at one of these events." Jesse walked over to Kendra's booth. A blond beauty, she looked like Miss Teen Rodeo or something with her bright white teeth, striking green eyes and nice-fitting jeans. Jesse complimented her on her cover art and looked over some of her other pieces. They chatted a short while about colors and images and the areas depicted in her paintings. Jesse shifted from side-to-side and found himself a little nervous, running out of things to say.

"Hey Kendra. How ya doin'?" Stella didn't wait for a response. "I just remembered I owe you a coffee. What cha doin' tomorrow? My brother Jess and I would like to buy you a cup." Stella set the date up for the three of them the following day, just like that. No hemming and hawing.

Walking out of the lobby, Stella explained that Kendra was doing some marketing work for the ranch. She thought Kendra was a very talented artist who just needed a break. After seeing her work, it wasn't hard for Stella to convince her bosses to provide Kendra the opportunity to work on a big project.

As they drove back to the ranch that night, Stella probed Jesse about his love life and what happened to his girl, Kerry.

"She's headed for big things and I didn't want to get in her way." Jesse didn't enjoy talking about the break-up. He wasn't at his best when he left her those many months ago, and they hadn't been in touch since. Friends let him know that she planned to be in Buffalo Ridge for Christmas in two months, but he just wasn't ready to see her. He would spend Christmas in Arizona.

JESSE AND STELLA met Kendra at the Pony Espresso Coffee Shop in town the following morning. Stella shared some photos she had taken of the ranch and cattle and a few someone else had taken of her. She looked right at home in the photos with a flannel plaid shirt, jeans and chaps. The photographer captured her beautiful face. Especially in the photos where she sat atop her horse, she looked like the boss lady of the canyon. Her boots showed years of heavy wear and her bandana was soft from many washings. She was the real deal.

Kendra explained the website design with its banners and videos, all of which was beyond Stella's level of expertise. Despite the busyness of the small coffee shop and the rising tide of voices, Stella listened while Kendra explained the various elements of marketing. The surrounding activity distracted Jesse, but he tried to stay engaged in the conversation.

"I trust you to take care of all this Kendra. I've seen your work, and it's fantastic." Kendra thanked Stella for her kind words as she jotted down some notes. "I just remembered, there are a couple more photos I meant to bring. I'll have Jess bring them in tonight. Are you available to meet him at the Rodeo Lounge about 8 tonight?"

"Smooth, Stella," Jesse thought. He wasn't sure how he felt about being set up by his big sister. He looked at Stella sideways through narrow slits but before Kendra could see he smiled and looked down at his coffee.

"Yes, I'm free tonight. I'll be there." Kendra had planned to stay home and work on some graphics but would accommodate Stella. Showing Stella she could do a good job was important. Besides, the brother was a good-looking cowboy. Not her usual type. Tall, dark, bad-boy cowboys were like chocolate to Kendra. She looked forward to spending time with someone outside that mold. Jesse's wasn't her usual eye candy, but he looked good in his jeans.

"What the heck, Stel. Why are you pawning me off on that little doe? You don't think she's got dates lined up on a Saturday night? What were you thinking?" Jess was only half-mad at his sister for throwing his hat into the ring. He knew he would not ask her out on his own. Being an introvert, he enjoyed spending time with himself. But since Stella lined up this date, he would be there.

"Nah, she's broke up with her no-good boyfriend. Besides, what difference does it make to you? You've got no love life." Stella needed to tease him a little. He blushed so easily with that fair complexion of his.

"Me? What about you, old little spinster on the prairie? You're married to those cows and canyons, aren't you?" Jess tried to pull some intel from his sister. He didn't know if she was seeing anyone. He hoped, for her sake, there was someone she could snuggle up to when she was ready to let her hair down.

"Now son, that's just really none of your business, is it? As a matter of fact, I do have a date tonight. With the business accountant." Stella changed from her t-shirt into a dressy western shirt and traded her sneakers for boots. Tonight was all about business. She knew the accountant needed to discuss some speculations with her, especially if they had to change herd size or lost the federal lease agreement.

"Oh great, a working dinner. Hope that goes well for you."

Jesse, too, was changing. He traded one t-shirt for another. Kendra would expect him to change from what he was wearing when they met up earlier in the day. It's just a thing some girls have.

They ran some errands in town, returning to the ranch in time for Stella to clean up and head to her meeting. Jesse quickly swept out his truck. There were all kinds of crumbs from his road trip and a pile of empty coffee cups. By 7:00 he was ready to head back to town, with enough time to find the Rodeo Lounge.

When Jesse realized that Stella had not given him the pictures for Kendra, he sent off a text. *Hey, where r the pics 4 Kendra?* Stella didn't respond. He tried calling and her phone went to voicemail. He rummaged around a little on her desk, to see if maybe she had left them there, but no such luck. He didn't have Kendra's number to cancel, so he drove to town and found the Rodeo Lounge. He took a bar stool and ordered up a beer.

Kendra looked hot - the kind of hot girl that could get a guy in trouble. Her red and white checkered western-cut shirt was tied at the waist and unbuttoned nearly to her navel ring. A red bra with rhinestone sparkles peeked out, as if to deliver a dare. Jesse tried to keep it to business. He greeted her with an apology as she sidled up next to him at the bar. "You're not going to believe this, but Stella left me high and dry. She didn't give me anything to bring."

"Want a beer Ken?" The bartender slid a glass of beer across the bar. Clearly she was a regular here. This bar was just another hometown watering hole. There were no quirky characteristics, just a collection of booths and tables and white-washed shiplap walls.

"I don't think there are any. She gave me everything I need." Kendra smiled up at Jesse and held her glass out to toast. "Here's to an awkward set-up."

Jesse smiled and shook his head. Stella would get a piece of his mind later, but since he had this beauty in front of him, he should practice his social skills. He invited Kendra to move to a quiet booth in the back of the room.

"Hey Kendra!" a table of cowboys, who seemed to have gotten a head start on the drinking, called out as they passed by. Kendra seemed to like the attention. She snapped her head and flipped her golden waves. Her shoulders inched back as she stood tall.

"Hey boys. Justin, does your wife know you're here?" She had already passed but threw the volley over her shoulder. Small towns. There are no secrets. Although it wasn't as small as Buffalo Ridge, Pascal had a small-town feel, at least from what he had seen so far. Jesse liked that. It was comfortable.

Jesse motioned for Kendra to take the inside of the cafe-style booth. She motioned back for him to take the inside. The red faux-leather seats were well worn. Clear tape attempted to mend the rips. He slid in, expecting Kendra to take the bench across from him. His breath caught, his diaphragm froze briefly and his muscles tensed when she slid beside him. Jesse hadn't been this close to a girl, other than his sister, for months. He felt a thrill with the occasional not-so-accidental collision of blue-jean-clad thighs as they chatted.

Kendra was a lifelong Pascalian and came from a ranching family. Her parents divorced when she was young. She lived in town with her mom but preferred to be at the ranch, even if only her stepmother was there while her father was away. These days she was working hard at developing her graphic art and marketing business. She had taken some classes but was not interested in earning a degree. They had that in common.

"Way I see it, there are lots of folks that never go to school and make a damn good living. I'm ready to start living and move out on my own. The sooner I can do that, the sooner I can do the things I want to do, like travel. Eventually I want my own place in the country but my folks would rather see me married and raising kids. Not interested. At least not now."

Another thing they had in common. They both wanted real-world experience before settling down. Maybe Stella knew what she was doing with this setup.

As they finished their second beer, Jesse looked around the joint and nodded to the door. He was ready to go home. Jesse asked Kendra if she was ready to go and if she wanted a ride, half-hoping that she would invite him over or suggest they do something else. He wasn't familiar with the area to know all the hangouts, but he was done with the Rodeo for the night. After just a few beers, cowboys could get unnecessarily lewd and strong. Also, he didn't want drive home after a third beer. Jesse wasn't a big drinker and could easily become disoriented in this unfamiliar place.

"Hey, my girl Sammi is over there. I'm going to hang here for a bit. Thanks though." She scooted closer to Jesse and threw her arm around his shoulder, pivoted square with his shoulders. She looked into his eyes and brought her nose close to his, begging him to put his face in hers. "Can I see you again?"

Jesse enjoyed his time getting to know Kendra but knew he had barely scratched her surface. They agreed to connect when he was back in from his next trail ride.

Kendra snatched Jesse's cell phone from his shirt pocket and snapped a picture of the two of them. She sent the photo to herself and created a new contact for her in his phone. "Here. Now you have no excuse. I expect to hear from you."

With a smile, she teasingly held the phone out for Jesse to grab. When he did, she rested her hand in his palm, interlacing fingers. There she paused for just a moment. For Jesse, the moment came with a certain thrill and he squirmed uncomfortably. Kendra hopped out of the booth to join her friends. Her hips and curls swayed in opposing directions as she moved away from him.

Jesse returned to Stella's dark home. Stella's dinner meeting must have run late. It was hard for him to settle. He was amped up from the little show Kendra put on. It was nice being close to a beautiful woman, if not a little unsettling. Jesse felt the urge to put some thoughts down on paper. He pulled the journal from his backpack and penned some reflections from his first days in Arizona. He wrote about the cattle roundup. It was unlike any he had ever taken part in. He wrote of his sister's cowboy extraordinaire persona, the poetry gathering, and Kendra, or more so his residual sensory overload from being around Kendra. Thoughts of Kerry came to him and he kept writing. He wrote about their courtship and their parting, laying out feelings he had never identified or shared before.

At his core, he was still very connected to her but his mind told him to leave her behind. He was on a new path now.

CHAPTER 9

*K*erry was excited to be at the ranch for Christmas. It had been a year since she was there and her soul longed to be on that familiar ground. School was going exceedingly well. She was happy to be working just one job now at the lab, with her heavy course load. She and Gracie took in another roommate to help pay the rent. Things were going well. She had even gone out on a few dates.

"Kerry, honey, it's so great to see you!" Her dad took her in his arms. She folded into his broad chest and relaxation swept over her. Someday she hoped to have a man in her life who she could love as much as her father. Someone familiar, kind, understanding, and caring. Someone who would be to her children everything her own father had been to her: encouraging, supportive, a teacher.

Her mother prepared her favorite meal of fried chicken, mashed potatoes and gravy with fresh baking powder biscuits. She listed for Kerry all the festivities happening around Buffalo Ridge in the week leading up to Christmas.

"The Buffalo Ridge Ranch has sleigh rides and there will be hot chocolate and music in the barn afterwards." Susan finished the list with news of this event. It had always been one of Kerry's all-time favorite things to do in Buffalo Ridge at Christmas when she lived there. But that was a different time. Kerry had moved on, or so her mother hoped. Kerry didn't talk much about dating but Susan thought maybe she just wanted to be low key. Certainly a young woman as beautiful and competent as Kerry would be sought after. Sure, Kerry wasn't a party girl, but still, she needed a night out sometimes.

"I should stop over and see Jesse. He'll be driving the hay wagon again I guess." Kerry had a nostalgic look about her as she mentioned Jesse by name.

"Oh, haven't you heard? Jesse is in Arizona with his sister Stella for the winter. He's helping her on a ranch that she works on." It surprised Susan that this piece of gossip hadn't gotten to Kerry. She realized that the chasm between Jesse and Kerry was much larger than she thought which brought a certain sadness.

"Some folks in Buffalo Ridge say Stella bit off more than she could chew and called home to get her brother to help. That girl always was too big for her britches." And yet, despite the gossip, deep within Susan felt envy.

Kerry was quiet. She hadn't heard. She hadn't reached out to Jesse since that day in May when he dumped her. Kerry finally read his book and wanted to talk to him, in person, about the things he had written. Beautiful, profound things that touched Kerry's heart.

Kerry quickly changed the subject. "Well, of course I want to go to the pie social and the cakewalk. Those church ladies know how to throw a party." In a small town like Buffalo Ridge, the church ladies are the social committee. "I would love to see Mr. Walker. Do you want to go to the Christmas concert with me?"

Kerry needed to dig into all the activities to avoid thinking about Jesse, who had been on her mind a lot since she decided to come home for the holidays. A dull gnawing started in her stomach when she learned he wouldn't be there, but for her parent's sake she would make the best of it.

The holiday activities exhausted Kerry. She and her mom baked cookies for the assisted living home, wrapped angel presents for the church, and hit every sale and bazaar in town. They took a day to have mani-pedi's at the local salon and chatted with the women there, catching up on all the town gossip.

"Have you been out to see Cathy yet?" the nail artist, Shelly, asked. "She's big as a house. Looks like she's having twins, but she swears there's only one in there."

Boy, Kerry felt out of touch. She hadn't been on Facebook for months and had called no one but her parents all year. Texts went unread and unanswered. She felt like a real looser of a friend.

"I had no idea they were expecting. How exciting for them," Kerry responded. "That was fast. Seems like just yesterday they got married."

"Right!" A familiar voice came from around the corner. Whitney peeked her head around and squealed. She rushed to Kerry, who pulled away from the manicurist and jumped from the chair to give Whitney a big squeeze.

Whitney had just stopped in to pick up a gift certificate for her mom and had to rush off. "On my lunch break," she quipped. "The Diner is calling."

They promised to catch up the day after Christmas, before Kerry left for school again. She had to get back to manage the lab. They were expecting shipments of new supplies for the next semester and she needed the extra money. When Professor Duncan asked her to work the week before New Year's, it was an easy decision.

Kerry skipped the Buffalo Ridge Ranch events. There was no need to look backwards, she thought to herself. She saw the Davies family at the Christmas Eve church service and waved from a distance but avoided them afterwards. She went home with her parents to enjoy their traditional chili dinner before opening one gift from under the tree. It felt great to be grounded and at home with her parents, even if only for a little while.

Before she went to bed, she sent off a text message to Jesse. *Merry Christmas (emoji Christmas tree with heart ornaments).*

When she didn't hear back from Jesse by the end of Christmas Day, Kerry felt sad. Was she so awful that he couldn't even wish her a Merry Christmas? She looked around her room and decided there was nothing more she needed to pack. She was ready to move on and leave all this behind her. For good. She would visit her parents, of course, but this town was too small. There were too many memories she needed to break free from.

THE NEXT MORNING AFTER BREAKFAST, she loaded presents and belongings into her car and hugged her parents goodbye. She had already spent time with Prince and Gypsy (who was showing her age) telling the faithful horse, "Here girl, here's a carrot for you. You hang out until the spring flowers rise and I will come back to see you." She completely forgot about her promise to visit Whitney.

As she drove away, she passed the Buffalo Ridge Ranch, sitting atop the bluff overlooking the Badlands on one side and Buffalo Ridge town on the other. Postcard perfect, she thought. A dream from the past.

By the time she got to the lab the following day there were boxes piled outside the door. She looked forward to keeping busy over the next week, organizing the lab and getting herself ready for the next year. She shook her head. Her unanswered text to Jesse was a sign that she needed to move on.

Gracie returned to Brookstone on New Year's Eve. She had a gymnastics meet early in the new year and the coach had scheduled practices over the holiday break. "The team is having a New Year's Eve party. There'll be no alcohol, no dancing, and no sweets. If you want to come, you can be my plus one."

"Gee, sounds like quite a blast! Think I'll stay home and read my syllabi for next semester and eat Christmas cookies."

"Right, that will be a lot more fun. Really, we get dressed up and drink sparkling cider. There will be confetti at midnight, lots of loud music and pizza. What've you got to lose?"

"My self respect." Kerry laughed with her friend. Gracie went to the closet and tossed a cute dress out to Kerry. "Here, hot stuff. Put this on. We're leaving at 8."

The party was a lot of fun and, on the plus side, there was no hangover the next day. There were about fifty people in the condo complex clubhouse of the community where the gymnastics coach lived in. The New York New Year's ball drop was on the big screen. Board games were set up on tables on the periphery of the room. They had decorated to the rafters with neon-colored streamers, disco balls, and strobe lights. A huge boom box blaring 80s music sat on the kitchenette counter.

"This place looks like they preserved it from the 80s," Kerry commented when they first walked in.

"Yeah. This is the coach's one big bash every year. She and her husband do all the decorating and cleanup. Apparently, they got engaged, or met or something on New Year's Eve and so it's become their thing." Kerry knew that Gracie loved her coach. Gracie described her as caring about the whole person not just the athlete. Kerry saw this when Gracie struggled early on, being far from her family, especially her brother Gabe. Coach and her husband included Gracie in some of their own family's activities and that helped Gracie through the rough spot. She went fishing and hiking with them and to several dinners at their home.

"Come on, there's an escape room game over there. Let's show 'em how it's done." Gracie and Kerry joined in the fun going from game to game all night. As the final countdown got closer, the whole room was up dancing. Kerry found herself dancing with a good-looking guy with dark hair, mysterious deep brown eyes and a tight body. Clearly he spent a lot of time at the gym. She had met him, along with about fifty other people, earlier in the evening. Mac came as a plus one with his sister, Jill, who was on the team. He had driven Jill back to school from Minnesota where he attended college.

Mac danced closer and closer to Kerry until he had his arm around her. At the strike of midnight, she raised her glass to toast this good-looking hunk of a guy. He leaned in and, without warning, planted a warm, luscious kiss on her unsuspecting lips. She let him linger a moment and pulled back to catch her breath.

"Um. Hello. I'm Kerry." She reached her hand out to shake his. He laughed.

"Yeah, I know. Your friend Gracie told me all about you. I'm Mac. Here with my sister Jill." He nodded toward a lean sandy-haired girl in the crowd.

"Oh yeah. Sorry, we met earlier. You just — um — took me by surprise."

"Sorry about that. I just like a memorable celebration. How about you?"

"Well, I will definitely remember this one. You're lucky I didn't reach up and slap you." Kerry gave a half-hearted laugh. He was lucky. Kerry liked her personal space and didn't give it up freely.

"Is that right? Well, thanks for not slapping me and I hope you have a wonderful New Year. And, that lip gloss is mighty tasty." Mac smiled that kill-them-with-kindness smile he had perfected and gave Kerry a light tap on her upper arm. "Forgiven?"

Mac didn't care if she forgave him or not but didn't want to leave any bad marks behind for his sister.

"Forgiven." Feeling awkward and out of place, Kerry excused herself and wound her way through to crowd, away from Mac, to find Gracie.

"Hey, you ready to go? I'm done with this scene." Kerry had an edge to her voice unfamiliar to Gracie.

"Sure, girl. Let me just say goodbye to coach." Gracie carried her heels in one hand and her sparkling cider in the other. She hugged Coach and her husband and wished them a happy New Year. Kerry waved and mouthed her thanks from the doorway. She couldn't get out of there fast enough.

"Wow, that was fun! It was good to see the team again." Gracie loved being part of such a close team. Unlike her high school days, she wasn't competing with her teammates as much as she was competing with herself. That's the environment the coach fostered, and it made each one of them a better athlete.

"What did you tell that guy?" Kerry was edgy, almost accusatory, as she tried to get information from Gracie.

"Huh? What? Tell who?" Kerry's questions confused Gracie.

"Mac. Jill's brother. He said you told him about me. What did you tell him?"

"Really? All I told him was your name. He asked who the gorgeous girl in the knockout dress was and I gave him your name. Why? What's wrong?" Gracie was worried that she had missed something. She looked her friend over. It didn't appear that she survived an attack or anything.

"He kissed me. Right there, in a room full of people, this stranger kissed me." The kiss obviously upset Kerry. There had to be more to it than this.

"Well, I know a lot of girls who would be flattered that a beautiful man like Mac, with his rippling muscles, bright white teeth and fashionable clothing, kissed them at the stroke of midnight on New Year's Eve. I'm not so sure what's got you all knotted up. Chill." Gracie had a great night and didn't want to come crashing down over a friend being kissed. It wasn't like Kerry to get so touchy about something that seemed so minor. Gracie made a mental note to bring it up when Kerry was calmer.

LATER, as she lay on the couch in the quiet, dark apartment still amped up from the evening, Kerry tried to unravel her feelings. She gazed out the window to the night sky for answers. She tried to see the situation from her friend's perspective. When she stopped to think the situation through, she realized her reaction was extreme. She did feel slightly flattered, but whenever she thought about kissing, it wasn't with a stranger. Mac was not her type. The only person she thought about kissing was Jesse. Getting over him was harder than she thought it would be.

CHAPTER 10

*J*esse and Stella spent Christmas week on the trail. It was Stella's tradition.

"I'm not a church-goin' gal, but I know when I am out here under this sea of stars surrounded by critters, wild and tame, that there is some good force greater than me making all this happen." Stella dug in her pack and pulled out a tin of Christmas goodies that a dear friend gave her. She passed the treasure trove of sugar goodness to Jesse.

Jesse leaned back and stared up at the indigo sky. A million pinholes of light dotted the darkness. He breathed in the cool, fresh air. He agreed that there was something in the vast unknown making all this possible. Something he couldn't touch but could see in the ordinary, in the eyes of those he loved, and feel in the touch of someone special. He had only met one person like that. Kerry. Somewhere out there was the one his heart longed for. He wondered if she was also looking up into the night sky, thinking of him. He shook himself out of his whimsical daze and looked into the warm fire.

Jesse stopped bringing his cell phone with him on these trips. There was no use. The cell towers were too far and few between to make it worth the risk of losing the phone. Stella carried a satellite phone in case they ever needed it for an emergency. Their mom and dad had that number in case they had to reach them. Stella brought her cell phone, but only to take pictures. She turned off the ringer and the data. She loved taking photos of baby snakes, spiders and every form of wild thing she could spy. Jesse had seen her share a photo or two with friends in town. He quietly pondered why she shared none of those photos or stories with their family. Maybe she didn't want to alarm Mom with pictures of black widow spiders or rattlesnakes.

When the eve of New Year's Eve gave way to morning light, they packed up camp for the last time that year. Stella threw some sage on the embers of the campfire. This was her way of cleansing the space, she explained.

As they rolled through town on their way home, they stopped for a New Year's Eve toast at the Rodeo Lounge. People packed into the place. It was impossible to get to the bar without risking an elbow in the ribs or a shower of beer from a mug.

"Hey cowboy, where you been?" Jesse looked down to see a very cute and tipsy Kendra walking by, holding hands with a guy. Jesse tipped his hat at her.

"Oh boy, that Kendra's quite the party girl isn't she Stella. Can't believe you tried to hook us up." Jesse gave his cute boy grin to his sister and shook his head.

"Just trying to do you a solid brother. Come on, this place is crazy. I've got some gut rot at home I'll break out."

Midnight was approaching as they kicked off their boots and sat their tired bodies down. Stella poured them each a smooth whiskey that Stella had held back for a special occasion.

"Here's to a beautiful ending to the old year and a wonderful start to the new. So glad to have you here, brother." Stella raised her highball glass to his. He agreed that it was a great place to be as they moved into a new year with a new beginning.

There was no rush to get up the next morning. Stella agreed they would have a few days off now, unless something came up, as frequently happens for a rancher. A new hired man, Joe Nance, joined them for some part-time work - checking the cattle as needed, fixing some fence and other odd jobs. He was another down-on-his luck cowboy that Stella wanted to rescue. She had a knack for that. Her skill for helping others seemed to be in how she held others, and herself accountable, Jesse noted. She didn't hug and smother. Instead, she set out achievable challenges and celebrated wins. Even small wins. She was a lot like their mother.

It was late morning before Jesse rolled out of bed, sore from sleeping so long. He threw on his jeans, grabbed his phone and stepped out of his chilly room into the warm living room. He had a dozen missed calls and some messages. Not unusual for the holidays and being out of signal range for a week, he thought. He set the phone on the kitchen table, poured himself a cup of coffee, and used the washroom. He was grateful for indoor plumbing on this chilly January morning. When he looked out the kitchen window, he saw Stella out in the yard cleaning up the tack and tending to the horses. Taking advantage of his official day off, he sat down to go through his messages.

Their parents had called him, a few times each, to check in and wish him well. He had text messages from his brothers and a few friends from home. One message stood out to him as he scrolled through them.

Merry Christmas (Christmas tree emoji with heart ornaments) from Kerry. His heart skipped a beat, and he felt a little tug in his gut, surprised but thrilled to hear from her.

Merry Christmas and Happy New Year to you. He wrote back finally after erasing many attempts at a more apologetic and detailed text. Jesse kept it short, clean, and simple. He didn't know what prompted her to reach out. Kerry was probably just being nice and sent this message to everyone in her contacts list.

Jesse checked his phone while doing laundry and helping Stella with the chores. He hoped for a response from Kerry.

"Hey, how about a New Year's resolution, you and I?" Stella tapped her brother with the back of her hand to get his attention. She had completed her chores and cooked them a late breakfast.

"What's that?"

"Let's get ourselves on stage at the cowboy poet's gathering in March. That'll be about the time you will be thinking of heading home. It's about ten weeks for us to write something up and hey, even if we flop, you know we'll be entertaining." Stella had thought about sharing a poem at the local gathering, but kind of liked having that part of her life as her own personal secret. Until Jesse opened that door.

Jesse had no confidence that he could write anything the least bit entertaining. He'd barely heard of cowboy poetry, let alone written any. Stella had a notebook full of material.

"Tell you what. I'll get in on this challenge but only under one condition." He wanted to see what she was writing. She had read a few lines, and he knew she was witty in her writing. He wanted to see whole pieces to get a better understanding of the craft.

"Oh yeah, what's that?" Stella wouldn't accept the challenge blindly. She needed to know what he had in mind.

"You share your notebook with me so I can get some ideas about what to write." If she was anything like him, there was no way she would just hand over a notebook filled with writing. It was just too personal.

"No problem, so long as you share yours with me. I see you. I know you're writing in that journal of yours." Stella had seen him writing late into the night by campfire glow and in his room at her home.

75

"I just write sentimental crap. It will not help you any. Most of it is incredibly personal. I am happy to share parts of it with you though."

"That's good enough for me. There's a copier there in the office." Stella nodded her head toward a large pantry converted into an office. She filled their plates with a hearty cowboy breakfast of pancakes, eggs and sausage.

Stella had ranch business meetings over the next few days. Things were going well for the ranch owners, Clara and Martin Drake. They were close friends of hers, but they were always thinking of contingencies if they needed to sell or could no longer manage the ranch. She enjoyed these meetings and felt respected as part of the brain trust they relied on.

"Stella, you've done a bang-up job for us again in the past year. We want to thank you for that. We've increased our herd size and have lost fewer cattle because of your diligence in managing them and the environment. Our government contacts have offered us continued leasing and lowered the price of the lease because of your fine work. They haven't seen anyone as successful as you in rotating the pastures and protecting the natural environment. Their fellas were out surveying in the past month and didn't see a problem with recovery of the scorched areas long term. Short-term, they think we should avoid them. Do you see a problem with that?" Martin had been in the cattle business all his life. He was a successful but humble man. He and Clara had a philanthropic mindset. They often cheered for the underdog. That's how Stella came to be part of their ranching family.

"I don't see any problem at all, unless you plan to double the size of the herd." They all laughed. Stella had long encouraged them to take on more cattle. They were content with what they had. Those that Stella managed, albeit the most difficult to manage due to geography and other natural elements, were not their only cattle. Based strictly on the head count, she managed about twenty-five percent of their overall holdings.

"One more thing, Stella. You have kept our overhead low by doing much of the work yourself. We want to share the lease savings we will realize this year with you. We are adding that savings to your profit sharing account. There is also a bonus for preserving the herd. You had a greater than one hundred percent herd retention this year."

"Yeah, it was so unusual to find that old bull out there this fall." She inadvertently added to the herd when she came upon this old bull in the canyon.

"Even crazier that he followed you into the sorting pens. I've seen nothing like it. He must have been out there a long time without being trailed. He's almost a pet now. We just let him wander wherever he enjoys going." Clara had told this story to many of her friends. They don't know where the unbranded bull came from or how old it was but he was content now to hang at the ranch.

"Clara, Martin, I want to thank you from the bottom of my heart for your generosity. Not only for this year but for every prior year. You know I love this place and would ask for nothing more from life than to be the cowboy I am. Not to say I don't still have things to learn." Tears came to Stella's eyes as the gratitude leaked from her. They were her family of choosing, the ones that raised her into adulthood.

"That's right. We never know what new tricks we will need to face future challenges but we appreciate you so and feel like we are the lucky ones for having you on our team. Clara and I will not be here forever. As long as we are, you have a job with us." Martin had pulled out an envelope. The documents inside detailed the day's discussion. Stella stood to hug them both.

They moved outside to tour a new stable on the Willow Rush Ranch. Stella met a new foreman for the original homestead sections. She was happy to see Martin slowing down in his daily work and letting someone come in and help him out.

Clara and Martin had only one child. He was born with heart problems that took him at a young age, before Stella knew the family. He was only eight when he passed but Stella believed they loved him dearly for the time he lived. Clara and Martin often lamented the fact that they had no heirs to gift the ranch to. They were sure that whoever received it would have the same love for it they did.

By the time they left for the trail again the following week, no messages had come in and none came in the following days. Jesse still hadn't heard from Kerry. Stella and Jesse planned to deliver minerals to the cattle. The grasses filled their bellies, but the cattle still required supplements. They hauled large bags of minerals and salt licks and placed them in strategic places near new grazing areas. Extra horsepower was required to haul the heavy supplements. They planned for just a few days on the trail, but as often happens, they got sidetracked solving other problems. This time they had to fix a fence that was no longer stable, and they came upon a cow that got bit by a snake and developed an infection. She roped the cow just to hold it still for inspection.

"It's odd there would be a snake up here with it being winter in the high desert but that fire probably impacted the animals." Stella smeared an antibiotic salve on the cow's leg. "She should be fine but we should watch her a day or so. I hate to see an animal suffer."

She let the cow go, and it wandered back to grazing, unfazed by the ordeal.

"She could also fall prey to the bobcats up here. A coyote probably won't tangle with her because of her size, but a bobcat doesn't care about that." Stella had seen it before. The smaller and injured animals were the most vulnerable. Instinctively, the other cattle moved in to shelter their injured pasture mate.

"Don't you wish people could be as nice as cows sometime?" Jesse commented on the nature of cows. He had observed humans to be so competitive and cruel to one another. He was thankful to be from a family that supported and valued one another and his parent showed respect to one another. They argued when the kids were younger, but they never called one another names. They always seemed to make up after they argued. As they aged, they didn't seem to have anything left to argue about.

After dinner Stella and Jesse sat near the fire and pulled out their notebooks. A lame cow could give them inspiration for their poetry. Or maybe not.

"I looked through some of your stuff." Stella pulled some photocopies from her backpack. "You are one talented dude."

"Nah, that's just me vomiting on paper. Just a jumble of thoughts."

"Seriously, man, if you haven't gone back and read this stuff, you need to. You write about the spaces between things. The thoughts we are usually barely aware of, if at all. You talk about the beautiful things that sit in the shadows of something that is bigger. This stuff is golden."

Jesse looked at his sister in disbelief. The only person he had ever shared his writing with before was Kerry. The one critic that mattered. She was so unmoved she didn't even mention it. Not even a courtesy, 'good job'. To hear his sister, whom he had come to respect immensely in the past few months, rave about his work was unsettling. Jesse hadn't read his own writing with a critic's eye. He dumped it on the page and then ran from it before it could swallow him up.

He turned to the next empty page and reflected on this day. A day filled with observations, surprises, and hope.

CHAPTER 11

*K*erry pulled a steaming cup of hot chocolate from the microwave. She set it on the Formica top of the classic 1950s dining table – a garage sale find she and Gracie fell in love with. The few craft supplies she owned and her *goals* notebook were spread out on the table. Her New Year's Day tradition started with a review of the prior year's goals. Sadly, this was the only time she reviewed them. Every year she promised herself she would do better. Realizing she hadn't, she clenched her teeth and let out a low growl of disgust with herself.

This ritual helped to organize her thoughts at an otherwise chaotic time. Last year she added a vision board to this annual exercise. Kerry had to dig through her closet to find it. A poster board with pictures and words glued to it. She flipped it over to start this year's visions. Gracie was at the gym and Chrissy, the third member of the apartment trio, had not yet returned from winter break. Kerry had the place to herself. There was nothing to interfere with her dreams.

A smile spread across her face as she looked over her goals from last year. Kerry had accomplished a lot! She was a half-year ahead in school after overloading her schedule every semester. She made the Dean's list and got good reviews on her job. Her bank account was in the black, albeit it barely, and she had kept in touch with her parents.

Kerry stood and folded her leg on the seat under her. She sipped her cocoa and looked out the window. Their apartment was the converted second floor of an old Victorian home. It stood in an older residential neighborhood within walking distance of the campus. Large old cottonwood and blue spruce trees were dusted with fresh snow on this winter morning.

She moved on to her less successful goals. The one sphere of her life that she had not accomplished, or made any actual progress on, was romance. This area was not typically her focus, but she had read an article recently. In '*Moving Through College and Beyond: Get these things right before you graduate*' the author stressed the hazards of not exploring relationships during college. Her theory was that too often women settled for the first man they dated after college because they feared that life was moving too fast. Kerry didn't want to settle. She added 'Relationship/Romance' to her list of goals.

To date, she had only two accomplishments in this area. She was kissed by a stranger on New Year's Eve and she sent a text message to Jesse. Really? One text message to a guy she had professed her love to long ago? Her new goals started with: call Jesse, today. She wasn't sure it would stay on the list, but felt compelled to write it. She focused the rest of her goals for the new year on school success and finally choosing a veterinary school.

Kerry looked around the apartment. The three college girls were so busy between work and school that they had never invested any time or money to decorate their apartment. She went to her closet and pulled out a cardboard box that never got unpacked when they moved in. She pulled out some pictures from her high school days. Her mother had framed and packed them for her when she moved from Buffalo Ridge. She placed them on the fireplace mantle to cozy the place up somewhat.

The first picture was of her and Prince at their last rodeo. They brought home the championship for their division. As they rode together, she and Prince were poetry in motion because of the way he took charge but responded to her shift in the saddle. Prince could run those barrels with his eyes closed, and she trusted him to bring it in fast and tight. He never failed her. It was only when she started getting in her head and doubting herself that she got off balance and threw Prince off. That was rare. She missed her dear friend. She didn't ride him while she was home for Christmas but she visited him every morning.

There was another picture of a friend she missed too. She and Jesse were sitting in a canoe on Gulch Lake. Their heads rested on each other. Buster crouched in the foreground. The blue lake with its tree-lined shore and an immense blue sky was behind them. This photo reminded her of something Jesse had written in his book to her. How long had he worked on that gift? She couldn't imagine. It's nothing she would even attempt to accomplish. "That's it!" she told herself. "Stop hiding and call him."

Kerry put off the call until late that evening. She warmed her mug of lukewarm cocoa in the microwave, grabbed a throw she brought from home and curled up on her bed. Why was she so nervous about making this call? Her anxiety increased the longer she put it off. She had been a bad friend to Jesse after he broke up with her and she was sorry for that. Finally she garnered the nerve to push the call button.

"Hey? Kerry? What's up? You okay?" A sleepy Jesse spoke into his phone. He wasn't too tired to recognize the number he had called thousands of times over the years. He had spent the afternoon and evening writing and napping. A rare day in this cowboy's world. He was wired to be up at dawn to get chores done.

"Oh. Sorry. It sounds like I woke you. What time is it there?" Kerry hadn't considered that Jesse would be sleeping.

"It's okay. Good to hear from you. It's somewhere between noon and midnight, that's all I know. How are you?"

How was she? Events had left her hurt, lonely, confused, excited, drained, hopeful, and so much more. Over all the noise in her head, what she noticed most was the thrill she felt at the bottom of her stomach. A feeling she hadn't had in a long time. "I'm good. Staying busy with school and work. How about you? I looked for you in Buffalo Ridge but Mom said you were in Arizona. How's that going for you?"

Small talk felt safe now. No reason to bare her soul yet.

"Yeah. I just decided I needed to get away from Buffalo Ridge and see what else there is in the world." Jesse wouldn't say he was running away from the reminders of her. He tried to flee his dream of them together after years of building a friendship and a budding romance. Those visions still intruded on his thoughts.

They chatted for nearly an hour just sharing their day-to-day lives. Kerry told him about her roommates, her job, and what classes she was taking. Jesse described the contrasts between life in Buffalo Ridge and Stella's world.

"And, she's the boss." Jesse shared how Stella spent days alone out on the trail with the extreme terrain and weather. He described how Stella managed the herd in the face of the forest fire breathing down on them. He told her how the owners gave her kudos. "It was easy to sit back in Buffalo Ridge and do the things I was familiar with day in and day out. Here, I'm learning something new every day."

"Wow Jesse, it sounds like you like it there and Stella's showing you a lot." She hesitated to ask the next question, afraid of what the answer might be.

"Yeah, she's amazing and Pascal, the nearest town, is cool too. We haven't spent much time there, but I met some local folks and hung out some." The excitement in his voice was palpable now. He had woken up, both this evening and in who he was becoming. It impressed Kerry that he was sharing so much.

"So Jesse, have you met someone special? You know, are you seeing anyone?" There, she said it. Scared to know the answer, she sat frozen while Jesse answered.

"Well, Stella tried to set me up with a gal. She was nice and everything but a little crazy. Not really what I need right now. I'm just kinda dating myself. Honestly, I'm spending my free time, uh, reading and, um, writing." He wasn't sure he should mention the writing bit. He was shielding himself from the critic he expected her to be.

That was it. She couldn't avoid it any longer. "Jesse. I'm so, so, sorry. I'm sorry I didn't read your book when you gave it to me." Kerry felt some relief that it was out. She was careless. She owned it. Now, to see if he would accept her apology.

"What's that? What do you mean?" Jesse wasn't sure he had heard her right. Did she say she hadn't read it or, was that her way of putting off the inevitable criticism?

"Well, it was a crazy time when I moved into the dorm and, well, there's no good excuse. I put it away and just didn't look at it. I thought it was something my mom had packed initially, and I had all I needed already unpacked and in its place. I'm sorry. I just totally forgot about the book until I found it again when I moved out of the dorm. Then it took me a long time to read it. It made me sad."

"Oh man, that's not what I wanted." Jesse sounded sincerely disappointed that he had inadvertently caused her pain.

"Wait, no, the writing didn't make me sad. I realized that I had my eyes closed to an entire part of you I never even knew existed. That's when I was hurting. That's what made me sad and even sadder still that because of my carelessness I didn't even realize it until long after you were gone." Kerry was getting teary now, thinking of the distance between them and her own haphazard treatment of Jesse's heart.

"Hey, Ker..." Jesse longed to take her in his arms and soothe her. This was not going like he thought it would. He had braced himself for a rant about the watercolor images he wrote in a black marker world. He expected criticism for the abstract way he described people and emotions. What he did not expect was the angst he was hearing from Kerry.

"No, ... please ... hear me out." Kerry took some time to compose herself, stifling sobs and pinching off her runny nose. She explained how self-absorbed she was and how she took him for granted. She expected that he would wait for her and, once she finished her education, they could start a life together. Kerry had not realized he had a passion for writing and that he was so very talented.

"Your writing moved me but I had to take my time with it. I wanted to read it, not like I was reading a textbook or a trade journal. It's like your heart was talking directly to mine, with no brain in the middle trying to translate. I'm sure that makes little sense to you but that's how it was for me. Even today, if I read one of your stories or poems I get something more out of it." Kerry didn't know how to describe her interaction with the writings. She never had the patience for literature before. She was accomplished with technical writing but she didn't feel that she had a creative bone in her body.

Jesse felt flattered, and a little hurt that it had taken so long for them to have this conversation. His gift was just, well, set aside, discarded. He tried not to focus on that. Just like there is timing in writing, he knew timing was important in life and his timing had just been off.

"Here's the good news. I think I've found an audience for some of my stuff. Stella introduced me to this Cowboy Poet's group." He wanted to - no, needed to - lighten the conversation. Kerry had flogged herself enough and now he had some, albeit dissatisfying, understanding of the months and months of silence around his gift.

"Really, there is such a thing? That sounds interesting."

Kerry wanted to be supportive but didn't understand what he was talking about.

"Yes, it's not like a poetry slam at the student union like you might have seen." Jesse didn't know if she had seen a poetry slam, but thought it would provide some context for her. "These guys work decades on their songs and poems because it's their lifetime of experience that creates the verse. The words don't just fly to the page; they carefully place them there after they've had broken bones mended, lost livestock and crops, delivered twin calves. You get the picture."

"That sounds awesome. I'm glad you have found some kindred souls Jesse. Arizona has been good for you." Kerry felt a pang of trepidation as she mentioned Arizona. She did not know if it was his new forever home or if he was just spending some time in Arizona helping his sister. She didn't feel it was her place to ask outright, given the time and distance apart they had.

"Yes, it has. I'm going to hate to leave it in the spring." It was true. Jesse was loving his time with his sister and this strange world of hers. He also had ties to his usual life at Buffalo Ridge. Part of him needed to be back at the ranch working in familiar territory.

"Oh, where are you going then?" Kerry hadn't wanted to ask but was glad it came up.

"I'll be back at Buffalo Ridge helping Dad with the calving. As much as I've enjoyed this time with Stella, I won't leave Dad hanging. Steve is getting busy with his new business and won't be as available to help." Jesse told her about Steve's dude ranch and Chance's nomadic lifestyle chasing rodeo after rodeo. Somehow he stayed alive and had a good time along the way, but being reliable wasn't his forte.

"I'm going to be in Vegas the last weekend of February through the first week in March. That's not too far from you, I think. Any chance we could catch up then?" Kerry just blurted this out. She had no intention of putting any pressure on him but it was true. The veterinarian she volunteered for would be there with some rodeo livestock and invited her along. It's an area of interest she had and it was a paid gig, so why not?

"That sounds interesting but at this point, it looks like I'm committed. Stella and I have a wager, of sorts, going. We will be tied up the first weekend of the month in Pascal. That puts us on the trail the rest of the month. Hope you have a good time in Vegas."

"Yeah, I get it. Thought I would just throw it out there. It's the same time as spring break so I won't be missing any school and the lab will be closed." Kerry regretted bringing it up. His excuse was probably legit but she may never know.

"Well, another time, maybe. I would like to see you and catch up. It's been too long." He wasn't sure how that slipped out. Now what did he mean by that? He didn't know if it was true but suspected it was. He hadn't allowed himself to think about it. "Hold on boy, you don't even know if she's available," he thought to himself.

"Jesse, I should get going. I've got to take care of some things around here tonight and get myself organized for the coming semester. I have lab supplies..." She trailed off, wondering what she was rushing off for, except that they had been on the phone a long time already.

"Kerry, thank you for calling. Would it be okay with you if I called you sometime? I can't promise it will only be on a Sunday." They both laughed sweetly. "We don't have great reception out on the trail and I usually don't even take my phone with me."

He felt fantastic talking to Kerry again. There was a lot to digest, but she was still Kerry. Still the girl that sparked longing in him, longing to be close and to plan a future with.

CHAPTER 12

$\mathscr{T}$he next few weeks, while out on the trail, Stella noticed her brother was unusually quiet. She didn't pry. She offered him a lot of thinking room. Finally she needed to confront what she recognized as unproductive internal dialogue.

"Dude, seriously, what is all this brooding about?" Stella slowed her horse down to let him ride alongside her. She wanted to hear what he had to say.

"Ha. Can't get anything past you, can I? All this time I thought you only read cattle." Jesse liked to poke a little fun at her reclusive lifestyle but he knew she was intuitive and read people as well as animals.

"Hey man, I'm a Davies too, you know. Our thoughts can be our worst enemies, especially if left to battle them alone."

Jesse shared his conversation with Kerry and his deep feeling for her. "Like you said, I'm a Davies but I don't always feel like one. I see you, Dad, Steve, all happy working your places and your herds…"

Stella interrupted Jesse. She could see the merry-go-round he was on and wanted to bring it to an abrupt stop. Jar him from his doomed thinking. "Don't you presume you know what's going on in anyone else's head!"

Stella described her real reasons for leaving Buffalo Ridge and the ranch. She met Hank, a hot, older cowboy, on the rodeo circuit. "That guy was a real heartbreaker. Looked great in jeans, dirty blond hair a bit longer than a girl's momma would like. A strong handshake to impress the dads and a sleeping room in a horse trailer lined with buckles he had won."

As she told it, Hank spotted Stella on the rodeo grounds at the Cheyenne, Wyoming Memorial Day Round-up. Before she knew it, his web of lies and swoon-worthy good looks had her trapped. He shared his big dream of living on the road. Hank wanted to travel from rodeo to rodeo, earning cash prizes and seeing the sites. He sat around the campfire strumming his guitar. He played tunes for the drunken crowd who didn't mind his lack of musical talent. Stella wanted to see more and Hank treated her like she was a grown woman, not Daddy's little girl who needed protection.

Hank, being ten years older, was much more experienced in matters of the heart, he said. He thought it would be a bad idea for him to meet the family. Instead, they developed a plan for her to tell her parents she was taking on a job teaching riding lessons to medically challenged kids for two weeks in July. Her parents would praise her for contributing to society. She used the name of a ranch operation they respected but had no business dealings with. She believed the coast was clear. So as not to be too obvious, she had packed only a duffle of clothes and her toiletries. She knew her mom would notice if she started emptying drawers and closets.

This is the first Jesse had heard about Hank and Stella running away from home. This chapter of her life was new to Jesse.

When Stella arrived at the designated meeting place on July first, Hank was not there. He did not show up for three days. She had arrived on the bus, leaving her pickup and horse at Buffalo Ridge. She had enough cash to cover a cheap hotel for a few nights, but couldn't hang out too long just waiting for him.

When Hank finally showed, he had a litany of excuses. His phone was dead, and he lost the charger. He had car troubles. He found a lost puppy and needed to find its owner. There were other excuses Stella could not now remember. She now found humor in his stupidity.

Hank was apologetic for being late and showered Stella with kisses and attention. For the next ten days they were on a road trip, destination unknown. Stella stayed in touch with her parents by text so they would be none the wiser about her shenanigans. They ate in diners or picked up junk food at truck stops, where they showered, occasionally. Hank pointed out landmarks and told her stories about various areas they passed through. She later learned the stories were all made up. He was a skilled storyteller with a sinister soul.

About a week into the trip, Hank announced that he needed to see a guy in New Mexico so they headed in that direction. They pulled up to a guest ranch in western New Mexico. Stella reached for the door handle and Hank stopped her. Told her he would only be a few minutes and she should wait in the pickup. He crawled into the sleeper part of the horse trailer and pulled out a canvas bag that Stella had not seen before. He carried the bag to a small house just behind the main building of the ranch. Stella liked this place. It was clean and homey and busy. There were colorful flowers planted in old wagon wheels and old watering troughs scattered throughout the yard.

The barnyard dog came to greet her. He sat outside the passenger door of the truck and summoned her to step out. She obliged. It had already been ten minutes and Hank still was not back. She wandered around the yard, visited with several of the trail horses tethered to hitching posts, between passengers she presumed. She wandered to the stable where she chatted with some workers. They were young, like her, and enjoyed working there. This was their summer job, before college started or between their freshman and sophomore years of college. She wandered back to the yard to wait for Hank. He was nowhere to be seen! He had taken off with the truck, trailer, and all her belongings. She checked her phone. There were no messages or missed calls.

"Hey. Girl. Are you here with a party?" A woman, about her mother's age, called out to her from the doorway marked 'Saloon'.

Stella approached the woman (Rachel was her name) and told her about Hank and asked if she had seen him.

"That no-good, lying, good looking, pain-in-the-a...." Rachel looked at Stella with pitying eyes. "Sorry honey, but that boy took us for a ride and we lost a bunch of money on him. Gary Raush, my husband, just run him off. We didn't know he had a gal with him. You're better off, anyway."

Stella told Jesse how the Raush's took her in and gave her a job. She never learned what Hank had stiffed them for but it didn't matter.

"You mean you weren't in college that year? I was a young then, but I was sure Mom and Dad said you were in college in New Mexico."

"Again, we are the Davies and appearances are still important. That's what Mom and Dad told everyone just to save face. I've never went to college until two years ago. I took an art class at Pascal community college to support a friend."

Stella poked holes in his vision of their perfect family. She was right. Image was important to the Davies family and things weren't always as they seemed. When he decided not to go to college, ever, his parents told everyone he was taking a year off. They said he would go to University the following year.

"I decided then, when Hank left me there, to take a stand for myself and never have to rely on a man again." Stella described how she stayed at the guest ranch for another year and it was on a horse-buying trip to Arizona that she met her current employers. The way she handled wild horses impressed them. They told her she was what they were looking for, and if she didn't mind working around a bunch of cowboys, they would like her to join them.

"The pay was good, and I was all business with the boys so it worked out well. I worked my way up in rank and finally landed this gig. I'm happy. And Mom and Dad never knew about Hank. They thought they hired me from the Wyoming job right into New Mexico."

"Hey, I'm not telling. That's your business." More and more Jesse admired his sister and her path to becoming who she was now.

"We started talking about you and your bad mood. How did I end up telling my story?"

Jesse smiled at Stella and rode off after a cow that was looking like she might stray. He needed to digest Stella's story. His mind raced with what a brave young woman she was and how she became determined to make herself something in a man's world. Then the inevitable happened - he started to compare himself and put himself down. Once a Davies, always a Davies. His mood did not improve. By nightfall he was too tired and sullen to write. The following morning inspiration hit and he penned some thoughts by lamplight in the tent. It was chilly in the canyon this time of the year. Sunlight broke the morning chill, and the workday started.

They worked through the day mostly in silence. Both were running lines and stanzas through their head. The cowboy poet's gathering was rapidly approaching. They struggled to write a poem they were both satisfied with.

"Would it be awkward for you if my poem featured you?" Jesse looked at his sister as they were driving to her place at the end of a long week on the trail. She looked as fresh as the day they left home, except her jeans were dusty. Stella confessed that she had wondered the same about him. She saw so much of herself in him and every line that came to her reflected that.

Ultimately, they decided they would do a joint poem for the gathering and it was a success. They worked through the lines together and finished with a masterpiece that neither of them could have accomplished alone. Jesse came to realize that, like Stella, he didn't fit the Davies mold. Unlike her, he hadn't found the gumption to break out on his own. That hesitation controlled his life. As the youngest son, Jesse was torn. Others expected him to stay home and help his parents. He wanted to build a life on his terms.

CHAPTER 13

The Cowboy Poet's Gathering weekend approached just as calving season at Buffalo Ridge Ranch was starting. Jesse knew he needed to return, if only because he had promised to help. He had learned so much in the few months he was with Stella and he hesitated to leave. She welcomed him to come back any time he wanted. A job would always be there if he needed one. The week after the gathering he would make one more ride with Stella to move cattle.

The lights were blinding when Jesse stepped on that stage. He had never shared his poems with a live audience this big before. He slid the sole of one boot across the stage floor a few times, trying to get his footing. Stella had been on this stage before. It wasn't the most intimidating thing she had ever done, but it wasn't completely natural either. She acted like a pro. She introduced the duo, talked a little about their ranch upbringing and their work together over the prior months.

They tag-teamed their poem that meandered through the twisted canyons of the area, drawing parallels from their lives. They drew laughs and breathless moments of tension as the story unfolded. The crowd received their poem with rousing applause. After several more poets and songwriter-singers performed, they joined the crowd in the lobby for a reception. Participant and guests alike complimented them heartily on their debut performance and the solid poetry they presented. Invitations came in to perform at community activities. They were invited to return to future local gatherings and a regional competition.

As the crowd thinned, Jesse saw her - standing off to the side, taking in the experience and looking at him with awe. Beautiful Kerry! Jesse grabbed his sister's hand to get her attention and excused himself. As he walked over to her, she quickly walked up to him and threw her arms around him.

"Jesse, that was amazing!" Kerry bubbled with excitement. She was thrilled to have seen Jesse in his debut performance.

Jesse couldn't believe she was there. She explained that after their New Year's Day call she surfed the net to see what was scheduled in Pascal that would have Jesse and Stella tied up. She had come over after her Vegas trip to surprise him and she was so happy she did. So was he! They had both been so busy that they hadn't talked as much as they had hoped.

Stella joined them. Jesse made introductions and Kerry swooned over the poem and Stella's presentation. Kerry had arranged to stay with the family of some friends from school. Jesse and Stella explained that they were leaving in the morning for some trail work. She was welcome to come to Stella's for the night so she and Jesse could catch up. Kerry quickly called her hosts and let them know she would not be staying with them that night after all.

Excitement pulsed through Jesse. He was high on adrenaline from the performance and his stomach fluttered when he saw Kerry. Her efforts to come to their performance touched him. They grabbed something to eat at Stella's and sat around chatting. Stella packed the last of the things she could in preparation for the morning. She set the coffeepot to brew at 4 a.m. and bid them a goodnight.

"Kerry, I can't believe you are here. It's just surreal." Jesse finally took Kerry in his arms and brought her close to him. He hadn't kissed her yet, and he was aching to. His eyes searched her face. Is this what she wants? She smiled, and he brought his lips to hers. Kerry noticed the fullness behind this kiss. The confidence. She allowed her lips to part. She felt his breath on her face and the warmth of his embrace. Home, she thought. I feel at home in this space.

He brought his face away from hers and continued to look into her eyes. That felt good, and he wanted more but he also needed to sleep.

"Do you think there's any chance Stella would let me go with you?"

"Seriously? Don't you have to get back to school?"

"This is spring break. I have another week before I have to be back."

"Tell you what. Be ready at 4 and we'll see what she has to say. You can take my bed and I'll sack out on the couch." After some protestations, Jesse had Kerry settled in his room and he lay on the couch. Restless. Confused. He was attempting to discern whether these were old feelings he was enjoying or something different. Before Jesse could resolve the question, he awakened to the sound of the alarm and the smell of freshly brewed coffee. He slid his legs out from under the covers. He was reaching for his jeans on the back of the sofa when Kerry came out of the bedroom. She was dressed, with her backpack slung over her shoulder. Kerry was ready to take on the world.

She spotted Stella in the kitchen and began pleading her case to go along. Stella looked at Jesse. He was watching Kerry with a smile on his face. She was tenacious. She always had been. It would be good for her to see this country. She may learn something from the unique ranching techniques. He hesitated to influence Stella's decision. She was the boss. The experience could broaden Kerry's view of ranching and cattle conditions. Who was he kidding? He wanted to spend more time with her. Feelings overcame him like a flooded valley after a downpour. He sorted and organized the feelings pulsing in many directions throughout his body.

Stella relented and sent Jesse out to prepare another horse. Stella knew, from conversations with Jesse, that Kerry could handle the trail. She was more worried about Jesse handling his emotions. He had grown so much in the last few months and was standing on his own. Stella didn't want to see him revert back to that lost boy that showed up on her doorstep. He allowed himself to be someone separate and apart from Buffalo Ridge Ranch and his father's shadow. Even if his journey of becoming took him back there, he would be a different person because of their time together.

Kerry felt like a kid at her first camp-out. She took in the craggy trail with its big boulders, fallen trees, high desert plants, all shadowed but colorful canyon walls. She commented on the similarities between the Badlands, Black Hills and this place. Kerry dramatized a collision of worlds. One was covered in pine trees with slate and limestone spires. The other landscape was like a deep bowl lined with colorful bluffs and tall molded clay shapes of the Badlands. When the worlds collided, they were transported to the desert.

The cattle intrigued her. Their unusual stature was different to what she was accustomed to, and they had a more passive, gentle demeanor. They moved deliberately, slowly, and were not quick to spook. The horses, too, were gentle, not pressured and sure-footed on the boulders and steep canyon walls. They found a calf struggling with a respiratory infection. Kerry was quick to take action and help the calf. She impressed Stella with her care. Stella was experienced in handling these situations. They got the calf stabilized and back on the trail. It had inhaled some noxious plant and developed a secondary bacterial infection.

The time flew by. With the extra help, they got everything done in three days. Kerry and Jesse had time to explore Pascal and enjoy extra time together. As the final day together approached, they both knew they had to talk.

Kerry shared her fears about showing up unannounced. It was a risk she needed to take. When she found his name on the roster for the cowboy poet's gathering while searching the internet, she knew she had to come. Especially after she had missed reading his book for all those months. She wanted to be on the front end of his success. She wanted to support him, even if he only wanted to be friends. That was a risk she would take. She loved spending the time with he and Stella out on the trail. It was fun and interesting.

Jesse told her he was returning to Buffalo Ridge Ranch for spring calving. He hadn't decided how long he would stay there. He didn't know if he would come back to Stella's. He wanted Kerry to know that staying in Buffalo Ridge was not a given for him. Jesse knew her heart was set on returning there and setting up a practice after veterinary school. As much as he had loved seeing and spending time with her, he just wasn't positive that's what he could commit to.

Kerry said she understood. She also said that single-focused goal was what kept her going. Her dad was sick. She thought about packing it in and going home to help, but her parents both encouraged her to stay in school and reach for her dream. When Kerry told her mother she was going to Arizona, her mother hugged her excitedly. "I know she wants something more for me. She tries not to show it but she always felt she would have had a chance for a different life if we would have lived where she could have pursued her own career."

Jesse listened. He took her hand. He told her that whatever happened in their future, he would always be grateful for this week together. Jesse praised Kerry's gutsiness for coming out, not knowing exactly what she would find. They agreed to stay in touch. At the end of the semester Kerry planned to visit Buffalo Ridge. Beyond that, neither would make nor request a commitment from the other. The ache that stayed with Jesse after their last embrace, however, belied his desires. Kerry roused his soul, and his body, in a way he didn't experience without her. He knew she felt the same way.

On Jesse's final day in Arizona he hung out with Stella, cleaning tack and helping her get ready for the next trail run. Stella praised him, like a mother hen, for all he had accomplished over the winter. She stayed away from giving advice about relationships and reminded him he always had a place with her if he wanted it.

"What should I tell Mom and Dad about you coming home?" They would undoubtedly want Jesse to tell them all about Stella and what her life was like. He needed to know what was acceptable to share. Stella told him to tell them it was their turn to visit her. In all the years she had been away from home, they had never visited.

Jesse snorted and told her it was obvious they were expecting her to crawl home. The bedroom she left all those years ago looked the same. Nothing had been changed. Stella laughed. She couldn't believe that the old stuff was just waiting there for her to come home and clean it up.

CHAPTER 14

*J*esse powered through the trip back to Buffalo Ridge Ranch. He stopped only for fuel, coffee and snacks. He was anxious about his transition back to the ranch and steeled himself for the barrage of questions he would get. Jesse also thought of Kerry. Sweet, capable Kerry. Those feeling he had once shelved, hoping to avoid, returned. Yes he loved Kerry, but did not see a happy ending with her because he didn't know what he wanted.

Yvette and Dan welcomed him with excitement when he returned to Buffalo Ridge Ranch. He told them story after story of his adventures with the ever-capable, and beautiful (no, she hadn't let herself go) Stella. He also shared a video of their duet poem. It brought tears to their mother's eyes. Even his father gave him a one-armed hug and told him he was proud. He didn't mention Kerry's visit. There was no need to create a 'thing' when they weren't yet sure what they were. He dodged questions about dating and the local Pascal girls.

His father shared a list of repairs and chores to complete. Steve had helped over the winter but was too busy to do the machinery maintenance. This became top priority. Calving started. Nights were late and cold as they stood by to monitor and assist if needed. Jesse took a notebook and pen with him. As he and Dad sat in the pickup while checking cows and calves, he turned on the overhead light and jotted down thoughts. He had written several more poems and possibly some lyrics. He didn't sing so he would have to share them with someone who did. When his dad asked him about his writings, Jesse just said he was writing about the cowboy ways. His dad could stomach that.

In fact, much of what he was writing had overtones of love in it. There was a woman. That woman took on many forms in his newest poems. Sometimes she was a woman. Sometimes she was a whisper on the wind. It was the look of love between a cow and a calf or the familiarity a horse and rider shared. It seemed to Jesse that the essence of a woman was woven into all of his writing.

When love came in the form of a woman, she was Kerry. She, his muse, inspired lots of thoughts. He tucked them safely in his special book. It stayed under lock and key. He blushed at some things he wrote.

The weeks leading to summer passed quickly. Jesse and Kerry tried to stay in touch but they were both so busy. They communicated mostly by text messages. Benign, 'thinking of you' messages. Jesse was anxious in the days before Kerry's end-of-semester visit. He didn't expect to feel this way. He was suddenly conscientious about how he looked and whether his truck was clean.

THE DAY FINALLY ARRIVED. Kerry promised to stop at Jesse's first. They both looked forward to catching up on one another's busy lives. Jesse cooked dinner, or rather served the dinner that his mom had cooked. His parents were conveniently out. They would not be distracted. Jesse showered and was setting the table as Kerry came knocking.

Jesse opened the door and there she stood, looking all grown up. She traded her jeans in for a skirt and top. She wore open-toed sandals with painted toes peeking through instead of the usual Ropers or trail runners. Kerry's hair, usually in a long braid down her back, flowed freely. She presented him with a bottle of wine. He laughed. He hadn't even thought of wine. What a nice touch to what was proving to be a perfect evening.

He reached for the bottle of wine, covering her hand with his. He pulled the wine, and the woman, closer. Jesse brought her to his chest, wrapped her in his arms and held her for a lingering moment before inviting her in. Kerry trembled as his strong arms blanketed her. She had been anxious as she approached the house, fearing Jesse would be cool toward her. They had not spoken much since their visit in Pascal. Her trembling gave way to something much more primitive. The anxiety melted as the yearning grew. It was good to be close again.

Jesse invited Kerry to join him on the porch where the table was set for two. He opened the wine and poured them each a glass. The spicy scent of the red-stained cork pleased him. The beauty sitting before him invigorated him. Kerry was all grown up, and it looked good on her.

The Badlands entertained them briefly as they sat on the porch. Rays from the lowering sun bounced off scattered mica creating diamond-like sparkles. Kerry pointed out areas reminiscent of those they rode through in Arizona. Kerry asked Jesse about his writing. He shared that he was writing more cowboy poetry and considering entering a regional gathering in Nevada in the fall. He kept his private musings to himself. Kerry was glad he was still writing.

She, too, had been writing. They accepted her into veterinary school and she was on the fast track to finish. She had to participate in research and writing up results. She could not stay in Buffalo Ridge more than a few days, as she needed to get back to her project.

"I've been thinking a lot about my week in Arizona and how different that life is. I have decided that I have a lot to learn about life and that was only the tip of the iceberg." Kerry was measured as she shared her thoughts. There was a lot more she wanted to say. She wanted to explore life with Jesse. Together they would make great things happen. She loved him and wanted to be with him forever. She was too afraid to share these thoughts. He ended their relationship once before and she did not want to feel pain from loss again. She also was not sure what promises she was capable of. She always wanted to come back to Buffalo Ridge to practice but now, she just was not positive.

Jesse agreed that it was an incredible experience. He also shared that it made him wonder what else he needed to explore. Jesse listed places he wanted to visit and experiences he wanted to have. He suggested Kerry might want to do that too.

"This feels good, sitting out here adulting, with our wine and our bucket lists." Jesse laughed, Kerry followed. He reached across the table and placed his hand on hers. "Thank you for taking the time for dinner before going home. I'm sure you're anxious to see your parents."

Kerry stood up from the palm tree cushioned wicker chair. She reached toward the glass-topped table to lift Jesse's empty plate. He gently encircled her wrist with his big hand and pulled her onto his lap. He took her face in his hands and brought his face to hers. He wanted to do this all night. Jesse gently and deeply kissed Kerry with her head cradled in the crook of his right arm. His left hand rested on her bare knee. Kerry felt the kiss - felt it throughout her entire being.

"Why, thank you Mr. Davies. That was the sweetest dessert." She swooned as their lips parted.

A car pulled into the yard on the other side of the house. They had talked so much they lost track of time. It was nearing 10 o'clock and his parents were home. They shared one more sweet kiss before piling the dishes and heading into the kitchen.

Yvette folded Kerry in a big hug. They chatted and giggled like two schoolgirls while Kerry cleaned up and poured Mrs. D a glass of wine. "Oh boy, you two are growing up."

Yvette had not thought of Jesse as a romantic pouring wine and serving dinner. It was time she stopped seeing these two as little school kids playing the dating game. Now they were young adults making adult decisions.

At the end of the evening Jesse walked Kerry to her car. They made plans to catch up again, this time at Kerry's home. Jesse had intended to see her parents when he returned to Buffalo Ridge, but hadn't made it over yet. They enjoyed another, longer, lingering kiss there, in the moonlight. The beautiful Badlands stood in the shadows. Ending the kiss was almost painful. The intensity penetrated deeply. Glittery stars danced above in the night sky as they whispered their good night farewells.

"I love you." Jesse whispered first. Followed quickly by Kerry's echoed affirmation. "I love you, too, Jesse."

JESSE HAD a lot to write about that night. Kerry slept restlessly in her childhood bed, her stuffed animals watching over her from across the room.

She awoke to the sounds and smells of her mother's kitchen. She greeted her parents with hearty hugs and joined them in their morning coffee. She noticed her dad was thinner than the last time she saw him. The spring sun had not yet bronzed his skin. Her parents were happy to have their girl home. She helped her dad move some machinery. Her mother shared plans to host several family friends that evening. A lot of old family friends wanted to see Kerry and hear all about her school and work. Kerry appreciated their interest. One day, they may be her patients' humans.

The day passed quickly. When the first guest arrived, Kerry was still drying her hair. She needed that shower to rinse off the dust and grime. It was good to see long-time friends, young and old. Kerry was wrapped up in her work at school. She rarely had a moment to think about life going on back here at Buffalo Ridge. She loved that familiarity she had with the townspeople. For them, there were no gaps in their adoration for the hometown girl. They loved her as much today as the day she left for college, even if they hadn't seen her often, or at all.

Kerry was in the kitchen freshening up a plate of cookies when Mrs. O'Connell popped in to get some ice. "It's good to see your dad looking so perky. It's been awhile." And with that, she left the kitchen leaving Kerry off-center. What was she talking about? Was there something wrong with her dad? Oh, there would be some discussion later on, she resolved.

The guests left and her dad headed for bed. Kerry stayed to help her mom clean up. As she loaded the dishwasher she mentioned the comment by Mrs. O'Connell and pressed for an explanation.

"We wanted to tell you together, but since the cat is out of the bag -- your dad is sick, honey."

"What kind of sick? Flu sick, stomachache sick — what?" Kerry knew sick and then she knew SICK. Her mother was worrying her with this vague response and Kerry suspected SICK was serious in this case. He was thinner, pale and tired.

Kerry's mom explained that he was quite ill. The doctors diagnosed him with stomach cancer, and while they caught it early, the treatment was wiping him out. The Brauns couldn't afford to hire help and she had been helping him as much as she could. Susan wanted to leave the rest of the discussion until morning but Kerry wouldn't have it. She begged her mom to let her stay home and help while her dad was getting treatment. Kerry would get a job and pay a hired hand. She would do anything so her dad could focus on getting better.

That's when Susan announced that they were selling the ranch. They had quietly made inquiries with some land auctioneers and realtors and were considering three different offers. "Your dad is heartbroken that he cannot pass this place on to you. That's all he's dreamed of since the day you were born." Kerry's eyes welled with tears. How disheartened her father must be. He has worked so hard all his life and this was the reward. They finished cleaning the kitchen. Kerry hugged her mother, long and hard. Her mother was a strong woman who loved her father immeasurably. This had to be hard for her too. Kerry went to her room.

Despite being physically exhausted and emotionally drained, Kerry was restless. She needed some fresh air to feel alive and clear her head. She sent a text off to Jesse. *U up?*

Before she could put her phone down, the response came through. She needed to talk to him. Kerry wanted to be with him. She didn't know if she wanted to escape the new circumstances or process the information. It didn't matter. She wanted him.

Meet at middle-way tree. When they were younger, they picked a place halfway between their homes where they would meet for bike rides, horseback riding or just to hang out. There used to be a tree there. That's how the spot came to be the middle-way tree. The tree burned down after a lightening strike five years before but they both knew the spot.

Jesse was already there when Kerry pulled up, sitting on the open bed of his pickup. She climbed up beside him and sat. Her shoulder leaned into Jesse's side as he put his arm around her, and she shuddered. He tightened his hold, reassuring her she was safe. No words needed right now. She would speak when she was ready. Jesse had heard rumors about illness and a possible sale, but he didn't bring it up with her because to him it was just rumor. He knew nothing for certain.

When her sobs subsided, Jesse hopped down from the truck and angled his body between Kerry's legs so he could look her in the eye. He massaged the tears into her face and smoothed her hair back. It was hard to see this pain in someone he loved. Jesse ached to take away the hurt and make things better for her. He knew she had to walk through this herself. He would be whatever support he could be to her. He had seen this kind of pain with Steve when Vikki got sick and died. He felt so much uncertainty, hope, fear and helplessness.

"I'm here. Whatever I can do to support you, I'm here." The words felt empty to him as he said them.

Kerry buried her head into his chest as she reached around and held onto him. That's all she asked, is that he be there. This would be a rough ride. She shared what little she knew in short spurts. Dad has cancer. He needs treatment. Selling ranch.

That last point struck Jesse hard. The ranch and Buffalo Ridge had always been an integral part of Kerry's dream. This wasn't just about her dad being sick. This news could change everything for Kerry! Jesse never saw this coming. He was certain she didn't have a contingency plan.

CHAPTER 15

*W*orking cattle and long days in the field kept Jesse busy over the summer. He helped Steve with the new dude ranch. Steve was prone to doing everything by himself. He failed to hire enough staff to help, leaving chores undone and phone calls unanswered. It was impossible for him to handle all the bookings, lead the trail rides, and prepare the chuck wagon meals. He hired help to clean the bunkhouses and do laundry but nothing more. His horse stalls needed mucking, the hay needed raking, and his cows needed sorting. Jesse pitched in with these things when he could. What should have been a big year turned out just average. They left tons of hay lying in the field.

"There is no way I'm making what your customers expect." Jesse picked up a soaking Dutch oven to clean for tomorrow's food prep. Steve said he had no complaints but finally agreed he needed help. He committed to finding help before the next season opened. Until then, he would see if Mom or one of her friends would pitch in. He was happy to pay someone to help.

Jesse built his own herd up through calving. He expected to bank a good profit later in the year. Long days in the field and on horseback over the spring and summer paid off. His wages were good for that work and his bank account was now decent. The earnings from working with Stella plus this year's crop and cattle cash gave him a nice nest egg. He thought about getting his own place. His dad would help him with a down payment if needed. Jesse wasn't looking for anything too big, just enough to call his own. His commitment to his parents and Buffalo Ridge Ranch were long-standing. He was in line to inherit the ranch property with his siblings one day.

Kerry visited Buffalo Ridge mid-summer to check on her parents. Her father's condition had stabilized some. He was not getting weaker and had started to gain back some weight. The neighbors pitched in, helping with the planting and harvest. Her mother's garden was producing well. It was unusual to see the garden peppered with weeds and in need of watering. Her mother spent much of her time nursing her husband. Kerry helped weed and prune.

It was important for the Brauns to maximize their profits for the year. They hoped to avoid selling but, if they had to, they would have a better foothold by finishing with a high-yield crop. In the fall, although the market may be saturated and prices only fair, the cattle would all go to market. For the first time in thirty-some-odd years they would own no cattle. They intended to maintain their horses, for now.

Kerry tried to be positive for her parents' sake, but she was crying on the inside. She walked around the ranch and tried to imagine someone else living here. The freedom to explore and ride the range she enjoyed growing up would no longer exist. Her precious Gypsy seemed to sense the upcoming changes. She became finicky in her eating and stayed close to the barn instead of grazing widely in the pasture. Prince was doing well, but he had taken to gnawing on the stall rails. He was bored. He roamed the pasture but was rarely ridden anymore. Kerry worried her horses would not have a home soon.

As she surveyed the landscape, a sense of foreboding swept

over her. Maybe Buffalo Ridge Ranch would become part of her past out of necessity and did not hold her future after all. She felt lost.

Jesse and Kerry spent the evenings together for the few days she was home. Standing side-by-side in the dude ranch kitchen, cleaning up the dinner dishes, was comfortable. Some nights they met at Buffalo Ridge Ranch, sat on the porch and surveyed the night sky for the rare falling star. Coyotes howled in the distance. This familiar place brought comfort. Jesse's presence eased her anxiety.

They didn't talk much; mostly just stared off at the beauty of the surrounding lands. They breathed in the essence of one another. Kerry held on to hope that her father's condition would turn around and they would not have to sell. Her mother was strong and positive. She encouraged Kerry to continue to focus on school. Kerry's education and reaching her goal were critical to her parents. They wanted her to succeed and discouraged her from changing her path to help them. Her mom also discouraged her from dragging Jesse into their family concerns. She suggested it was a conflict of inter-est, since Jesse's dad had placed a bid on the property. Jesse never mentioned this and, Kerry suggested, probably knew nothing about his father's business dealings regarding the Braun ranch. If he had bid, Kerry thought it would be a fair bid. He knew the value of the property and had longstanding ties to the family.

Jesse continued to show Kerry support but, as the summer wound down, he thought about what he would do in the fall. He considered working again with Stella or trying something else entirely. Kerry would tell him to do whatever made him happy. He struggled with doubt and wondered if he was good enough for Kerry. Was he scared to be her port in the storm for fear he, himself, would end up underwater?

Jesse wrote when there was time. His thoughts and his writ-ings turned to the future. Not next year, or the year after, but one, two and three decades into the future. He brainstormed ways to replicate portions of the ranching model Stella worked under. An idea sparked that he could also start a local Cowboy Poet's Society. Maybe Steve could integrate readings into his chuckwagon dinner show. His mind raced with ideas. Excitement returned as he envisioned future possibilities.

By the time Kerry went back to school, she and her parents had devised a plan. Her parents would move to the nearest city before winter and they would lease the ranch house and property, for now. They could manage the payments on the equipment for a while with the lease payments coming in. They had saved and invested for their retirement so they were not without resources. The end-of-year crop and cattle sales should be good. There were several bins filled with older grain that would go to market too. Kerry was much more settled when she went back to school but she still felt as if the underpinnings to her dream were coming undone.

On their last evening together, Jesse picked Kerry up and drove south about ten miles to the big Badlands. There, they sat on the tailgate and looked out onto the rugged beauty of the place.

"Jesse, you haven't said much. What's going on in that head of yours? Or, do I need to read your journal?" She teased, knowing how sacred his writing privacy was to him. She hopped down and squeezed herself between his legs. Nose to nose now, she had his attention.

Jesse was lost in thought as he imagined cattle moving through the Badlands, freely grazing where the wild grasses grew. He took her in his arms and pulled her close, gently kissed her beautiful face, then her lips. His heart swelled.

"Sorry. I was thinking about cows." He was intentionally unromantic, but honest. He wanted to be certain he had her attention. "Kerry, I love you. Someday, I hope... I hope we have a life together. Right now, we both have things to do. By my count, you have about three years of school left. That gives me time to get my shit together."

He needed to be honest. He wasn't ready and now, when she was vulnerable, she might want more.

"I love you too, Jesse. Thank you for being there for me this week. It's been hard." Kerry wasn't disappointed. She was exhausted and looked forward to getting back to school. Work and school were easier than the rest of life sometimes.

Kerry wandered across the clay table they parked on. She gathered wild sage to dry and burn. She liked the smell and felt it cleared the air and improved her concentration. Kerry had few rituals in her life. This one brought her home in spirit and that had meaning for her.

Their final parting was sweet, filled with kisses and long hugs. They made no promises to do anything but take care of themselves. Jesse offered to be there for her parents if there was anything he could do. "I'm proud of you Kerry." Jesse whispered in her ear. Those words meant more than anything to her in that moment. She carried them with her and called them from her memory many times over the following years.

JESSE WROTE into the early morning hours. With pen to paper he brainstormed a vision for his future ranch operation. His out-of -the-box thinking brought inspiration. He woke early, after little sleep, still excited. Stella was within cell tower range and answered on the second ring. Jesse pumped her for information on alternative ranches, like the one she worked on. He needed to know who else was operating outside what they grew up with.

Stella had some ideas of ranchers he could talk to. Throughout the day his phone buzzed as new contacts came through from Stella. There were about a dozen operations she had connections with. She had already reached out to several who agreed to talk to him.

He sat at his computer that night and organized a spreadsheet with his questions across the top and the names of the operations down the left-hand side. He sent emails to each of the contacts with proposed times during the week to interview them over the phone. By the end of the following week, his spreadsheet was filled, and he had additional pages of notes from his conversations. In some strange way, not going to college was having a benefit. He was not married to book learning and allowed himself to look beyond what he had always known.

"You are the best sis!" He started a long email to his sister. A text would not suffice this time. He shared his success in reaching each of her suggested contacts. Collectively they provided immense amounts of information that gave him food for thought. He closed with a plea to visit her, not for the winter this time, just for a few weeks when she needed help. This would cover the expenses of his trip, at least. He planned to visit some other operations he learned about as well. He would share those details with her when they were finalized.

Jesse looked back over the past few years. He remembered how he was as a lanky kid, a misfit in a family of notables. Today, he knew his worth. He was a success in his own right and was launching himself on a path to expand. Kerry was his constant. Even when they were apart he thought of her, dreamed of her, and longed for her. They had reached a new place together as they each worked to better themselves. Life was good.

Stella assured Jesse he was welcome to come back. They agreed on a time when she was moving the herd and her hand was unavailable. It also just happened to coincide with a Cowboy Poet's competition. They committed to work on another poem, drawing from work they previously started and refining it.

Jesse was gone nearly two months between his time with Stella and his visits to ranch operations in Montana, California, New Mexico and southern Arizona. He acquired draft business plans, copies of lease agreements and other materials to consult while drafting his own plan.

He enjoyed the time with Stella. She was steadfast in her work and commitment to her bosses. Stella managed to talk them into an additional twenty head on the range. She was charged with carefully monitoring the environment to ensure there was no overgrazing as a result of the increase. Jesse thought she had softened some around the edge. Her commentary was a little less biting. He couldn't put his finger exactly on the change, but something was different.

Once again, their performance at the Cowboy Poet's gathering was well received. Their poem featured a down-on-his-luck cowboy whose chaps were short and loops were long. His sombrero was wide and his rag too narrow. This poor cowboy didn't fit in anywhere. Finally, he hitched a ride out of El Paso in a low rider heading for Nogales. He learned to gangsta rap and now he performs at a comedy show in Vegas. The crowd roared when they heard the rap lines in the stanza.

CHAPTER 16

"*Oh* baby, you look so fine." Jesse was practicing lines for a new poem, standing in front of his bedroom mirror. His mirror. His bedroom. Jesse wasn't much of a housekeeper, but as he looked around, he wasn't disgusted. The place had a utilitarian, minimalist vibe going. His mother helped him do the deep cleaning before he moved in and his parents donated much of the furniture. It was timely for his mother to do some redecorating so they had some extra stuff.

Besides his tack, boots, and winter gear, his own belongings fit in three boxes and about twenty hangers. Two of those boxes were books. He did not posses anything soft and cozy to warm up the ambiance of his new-to-him home. Kerry sent him a house-warming gift from school. It was a stadium blanket in her school colors. The blue and yellow clashed somewhat with the burnt orange plaid couch but one day it would all come together. Today, it didn't matter.

The one big and special purchase for himself when he moved was a writing desk. Rather unconventionally, he placed it under the picture window in the front room. There, he has the best view of the plains and the baby Badlands. He didn't have the grandiosity of his parents' view, but the change in perspective was good for him and his writing. His prose took on its own unique character. His voice was colorful, weaving in textures and hues from nature. He was also empathetic and courageous in his verse. The glue for his writing was humor. Not the wit that oppresses, but levity that laughs in the face of everyday life.

His acreage was small, but it was a start and it butted up against his parents' ranch. Dad was cutting back as he toyed with the idea of retirement and had leased some land to Jesse. His parents took Stella up on her challenge and visited her over the winter. They only stayed in the Pascal area for a few days, preferring the warmer climate in the southern areas of the state, where they had snowbird friends. Stella hilariously described the confounded look on their father's face when she told him she was the foreman for the ranch and around there they call her a cowboy. She did everything the guys do, but sometimes with more grace.

"I was tempted to tell them all about Hank too, but thought that reveal was best left under cover. There is nothing to gain by telling them I lied and deceived them and nearly found myself in a terrible situation with a not-so-nice guy. Anyway, they were content to see that I was alive and well. We even went out to dinner one night, and I brought a date."

"No way! Tell me more." Jesse was curious now and shocked that his parents had said nothing about this new development.

"Sorry hun, gotta run. Catch up later." Stella was not in the mood to open that can of worms right now. What had started as a joke was turning into a nightmare for her.

Jesse struggled to decide whether to lay down roots here or take his show on the road, but ultimately decided he could do some of both. His last trip to see Stella was only three weeks long. He checked the cattle with her and helped to fix some fence, but mostly they just hung out and talked. She was more relaxed than before. They also took part in the Regional Poetry

Competition; they didn't win but made a good showing. There, amongst the boulders, the canyon and the undistilled wildness, he had a clear head for writing. He wrote and wrote into the wee hours of the morning when they were on the trail. He brought a headlamp this time. He could adjust it to reading light level, which was quite effective for writing without disturbing Stella.

Now Jesse was running his own modest herd of cattle and training horses. He had a few hundred acres of crops with plenty of hay for himself and some for sale. His lease payments were manageable and his parents were there for a cushion which he hoped he never needed. He held onto thoughts of approaching the feds about leasing some grasslands, but was happy with the size of his operation and the opportunity to pursue other interests.

His brother, Chance, was home regrouping and recuperating from injuries suffered during the last rodeo season. As he healed, he could help their parents on the ranch. The forced rest seemed to be good for Chance. He showed a new respect for Jesse and all that he had accomplished in recent years. He liked to tease Jesse about his poetry, but Jesse believed that in time he would develop a greater appreciation for that part of his life as well.

Steve followed through with his promise to bring in extra help. He got more than he bargained for when he brought in a cook who brought her young son with her, all the way from New York City. Jesse was too busy to spend much time with them but he was sure there was a story there and eventually he would get it out of Steve. Meanwhile, he was grateful not to be the dude ranch cook anymore, although he helped with trail rides and roping lessons occasionally. Vikki's greenhouses were still running with a local gal managing that. The dude ranch business took off and Steve just couldn't handle it all.

The one thing missing for Jesse was his life partner. He knew, finally, that he wanted Kerry to be in his life for the long haul. Jesse had pursued his own thing and while it felt great to be up on that stage and recognized for his creative work, that would not keep his bed warm at night or wash away his tears when the hard part of life came. He wanted to be building a life with someone and Kerry was the someone he knew and trusted to be that partner, long-term. He wanted to make that happen, for them.

CHAPTER 17

*J*esse brightened when he saw Kerry's father looking so well. He greeted him warmly with a firm handshake. Up close Mr. Braun looked older, but well. He had color back in his face and had stopped losing weight. And he looked happy and content to be back in his own home, away from hospitals and infusion centers. Although now retired, he loved being at home where he could watch the livestock and the changing colors of the Badlands.

"Come on in, son! How ya doin?" Kerry's dad ushered Jesse into the kitchen and poured him a cup of coffee. "Whatcha up to today?"

"Well, sir, I'm here on some important business." Jesse had written about how this moment might feel. He was anxious and excited and, well, more confident than he thought he would be.

"If it's about the ranch, we have taken it off the market." Kerry's dad, feeling somewhat irritated, picked up his coffee mug and took a big swig.

"No sir, it's not about the ranch. In fact, I am so happy to see you back here." Jesse looked at Kerry's father and gave him a big smile. "It's about your daughter."

The tension fell from Mr. Braun's shoulders and he took a deep breath. He had learned a lot about the dangers of stress and practiced meditation as part of his new healthy living program. The practice came in handy at moments like this.

"Oh, I see. What's on your mind Jess?" Kerry's father knew this moment was coming. The kids had finally found themselves. As Kerry was soon coming back home to start her practice, with Jesse's help, this visit was not a complete surprise.

"Kerry and I have had quite a journey over the last few years and I would like to make it last. With your permission, I would like to ask her to marry me." Jesse felt his hands in autonomic nervous motion. Until this moment, he hadn't expected that Kerry's dad might say 'no'.

Kerry's father furrowed his brow and told Jesse about his own bid for Kerry's mother's hand in marriage and how her father had put him to a test before he would agree. He had to sleep outside, by the White River, where legend had it souls would visit under the full moon and re-enact a war between the Native Americans and settlers. "So, I've been thinking about this and I have a challenge for you too. If you pass the challenge, you have my blessing."

Now Jesse was nervous. What on earth could her father have in mind?

Kerry's father continued. "There's a fundraiser coming up for a dear old friend of mine, Albert Harnisch. Seems he went and caught himself some cancer too and he needs to have some fancy new treatment that his insurance won't pay for. Anyway, I know your mom and dad have made some donations. I want you to come and read one of your poems at the event. Invite all yer friends on that app thingy you kids use. There will be lots of great stuff for sale and we need lots of folks showin' up."

Jesse had shared none of his poetry or writings with Kerry's parents. Sure, he mentioned that he and Stella had done some readings. His mind was racing through his writings to see if he had anything that would work.

"Oh sir, now you're making me stretch. I might prefer the night on the river," Jesse spilled and let out a nervous laugh. "But I would try walking on water to get your blessing, so I will be there, for sure."

He gulped down the last of his coffee and stood to leave. He shook Kerry's father's hand and thanked him for the chat.

THE EVENT WAS LESS than two weeks away. He needed to get to work. Jesse talked to some locals who knew Albert and gathered their impressions. Within days he had written a poem that captured not only the essence of Albert as he had heard it from others, but the commitment of his friend, Kerry's father, who promoted the fundraiser.

Work still had to be done, so time to refine the poem was limited. The town celebration was rapidly approaching and Jesse planned to help with several of the activities, besides performing at the fundraiser. Kerry was returning from veterinary school with plans to study for her licensing exam at home. But she would definitely be at the fundraiser with her parents and go for a beer with Jesse afterward. He had been so supportive throughout school and chasing her dreams; she wanted to share her appreciation for him. And she honestly missed him when they weren't together! His presence alone was refreshing, as it broke that singular focus on her education, and now career, and allowed her to just relax and enjoy life.

Jesse stood in front of the mirror. He examined his hair and his clothes - just to make sure he wouldn't offend anyone, his mother in particular. He smiled, not out of vanity but to be certain there was no spinach left between his teeth. Satisfied with his appearance, he headed out to his truck and turned to retrieve his notes off the seat.

He had rehearsed this poem, "The Taming of Albert O'Leary" two dozen times. If he had more time, it would be twice that before he ever presented it on stage. Jesse experimented with inflection and pace. That's what made him a great cowboy poet. He hadn't been at it as long as most; he took the time to polish every piece he presented. He had gotten so good now that he had a whole book of poems published, "Riding the Range, Backwards and Uphill." Jesse incorporated wit and humor in all of his poems, although some have a more serious overture of loss woven in.

He had other things on his mind too. Kerry was not aware of this yet, but he had framed and walled in her new clinic. In fact, no one in either family was aware he was working on that project. Since moving into his own cabin, Jesse found he had free time that previously was spent hanging out with his parents. Now, he saw them less frequently but made each visit meaningful.

Tonight Jesse hoped to hit two home runs. When he arrived at the venue for the fundraiser, there was already about a hundred people there, nearly all of whom he knew personally. He had shared a draft of the poem with Albert earlier in the day so he had a heads-up on what was coming. As Jesse approached Albert, Kerry and her parents entered at the front of the hall, Albert stood, weary and weak but with a smile on his face, and put his hand out to shake Jesse's. "You are a mighty talented lad there, Jesse. Who knew old Davies could raise such an artist."

The group laughed together. Jesse took a seat beside Kerry who gave him a quick kiss on the cheek. She whispered in his ear, "You've made him a very happy man, Jesse Davies."

She pulled back, looked into Jesse's eyes and smiled. Jesse raised his eyebrows and gave a slight grin. His nerves were starting to get the better of him.

He looked around the room. Townspeople had filled

tables with arts, crafts, and other donated goods for the silent auction. "Did you find anything to bid on?" he asked Kerry.

"Not me, but Mom has her name on all kinds of things." She nodded her head towards her mother who was going from table to table to check on the status of her bids, upping the amount if she had been outbid on those items she wanted most. As 7:00 rolled around, folks had finished eating their spaghetti dinners and were taking their seats in the presentation hall. Albert's daughter was the master of ceremonies. Jesse knew her as one of his brother Chance's classmates. They even dated a little. Well, Chance dated all the girls a little, or so it seemed. Another small town hazard.

"Folks, folks, can I have your attention, please." Patti stood up on the stage, a baby on her hip and husband by her side. She thanked everyone for taking part in the evening's fundraiser, introduced her father, named and thanked all the donors for the event. Finally, she held up a book with a cover that looked all too familiar to Jesse. Now where did she get that? It was a signed copy of his book of poems and she was introducing him. Apparently, his mother had donated one for the auction.

As the applause died down, Jesse took a long glance at Albert, leaned forward into the hand-held mic, bent his knees and started. He told a tale of a young man learning his way around the ranch on a summer job with his uncle, having been sent from the city by his mother to be 'tamed'. She told him if it didn't work, she would sell him to the O'Leary family. Now, he was just a boy of eight and an only child, but his mother was a widow and had to work so she wasn't around much to keep him in line. She couldn't afford a switch or a belt and had long since broken the wooden spoon, or so the story goes. At the end of the summer, they decided that he would stay with his uncle, who had a big family and could use the help on the ranch. Eventually his mother also moved to town and took a job. Albert, as a teen, saw a spunky girl that matched his wits and sparked his interest. He knew she would be at the country dance and he got permission to go.

As luck would have it,
his horse came up lame.
His truck wasn't fit
so he rode in with a dame.

Millie was there,
all gingham and lace
Her ringlets were bowed,
The rest of her - grace.

Albert tipped his hat and asked her to dance,
The poor little girl didn't stand a chance.

He trampled her toes and got caught in her lace.
He got a black eye when she slapped his face.

Now Albert and Millie,
they managed to wed
They birthed in a filly,
and built her a bed

The poem shared highlights and funny stories of Albert's life, talked about his illness and ended on a high note.

If you're new to these parts,
fear not what you hear
For Albert and Millie
are now raising deer.
At Christmas he rents them,
to PhotoShop with your tree
That's what happens to minds,

The crowd rose to their feet, in honor of Albert and praise for Jesse's tribute to him. In this community, everyone was supportive of each other. There may be spats over fence lines and such but when it all boils down, they are like one, big, happy, dysfunctional family.

After greeting new fans and shaking hands, Jesse walked up to Kerry's dad, pulled him close and quietly asked him if he had passed. When he got the thumbs up, he looked to Kerry's mom and said, "It's on!"

With that, she sprung into action and walked around the room, leaving Kerry's dad perplexed. Now for to the second home run!

Since they hadn't any bids in, Kerry and Jesse headed to the local watering hole to see if any friends were hanging around there. Several folks they met on the street congratulated Jesse on his entertaining performance. The bar was crowded, so they stood and chatted with friends they hadn't seen for a while. It wasn't long before Jesse became restless.

"Hey Kerry," he spoke quietly into her ear. "Your folks asked me if I would give you a ride home since they were going home right after the auction. I'm feeling somewhat beat since the adrenaline rush..."

"Hey, it's ok. I'm ready to head home too. I have more studying I want to do tonight." And she did. Kerry was bound and determined to take her licensing exam once, and only once, and then get on with setting up her practice. Other than the few conversations with Jesse about ideas for the clinic she would eventually set up, she had made no plans. Of course, she had taken a business class in school and had lists of essentials she would need, preferably used in order to keep within her currently non-existent budget.

It was dark, and the sky was moody with clouds partially covering the otherwise bright moon. Kerry walked around to the driver's side with Jesse so she could rub thighs with him in the pickup as they made their way to her house. Before she got in, she turned to face him, wrapped her hands around his neck and pulled him close. She planted a warm, luscious kiss on his lips and closed her eyes to take in all the excitement of the night. This man. This poet. He was hers and she loved him.

"Hey sweet thing, what was that for?" Jesse knew she didn't need an excuse to kiss him, but this was a very enthusiastic kiss indeed, more than just sweet.

"You continue to amaze me, Mr. Davies. I am so proud of you and am so grateful you are not hiding all that talent you have. Thank you for helping my pops out. He respects you a great deal."

She doesn't know the half of it, Jesse thought to himself. "Scooch your cute little self in there."

He gently guided her in the shifter's direction. There were people waiting, and he didn't want to lose momentum.

As they drove to the edge of town, Jesse took one turn before the turnoff to Kerry's ranch.

"Hey there, where are you going?" She looked up at Jesse and nudged him, just to be certain he was awake. He twitched when she poked him in the ribs. Kerry knew this country like the back of her hand and she knew he did too. Why would he make a wrong turn?

"I was working over there on the McHenry place and I think I might've left the lights on. I just need to run by and check." The McHenry place was between their parents' ranches. The Davies owned most of the surrounding land, but for the longest time the McHenry family would not sell the old cabin even though it had been abandoned decades before.

"Really? What's going on at the McHenry place?" Kerry was curious. Her parents hadn't said a thing about it and she hadn't been by there for years.

"Ah, just a local fella puttin' up a building I'm helping him with."

Kerry thought it was pretty strange. Jesse knew she would know whoever this 'local fella' was, but she didn't want to push it. He seemed distracted, and it had been such a good night. Why rain on his parade?

When they pulled into the yard of the old cabin, the fields around were pitch black but there was indeed a building there with its lights on.

"Grab that flashlight in the glove box. Let's go get them lights." Kerry reached into the glove box and found the flashlight. It didn't work. Jesse had disabled it earlier in the day. He didn't want her shining it around the dark field to discover there were about thirty cars parked out there behind the dilapidated cabin. He took her by the hand and pulled her along. When he got to the door, he patted his jeans to make sure his surprise was still stowed safely away.

"Wow, this is an interesting place out here. What's he going to do with it?" Kerry could see the outline of the building with the light shining through the windows. Jesse opened the door and Kerry jumped back as the group of familiar faces yelled, "Surprise!"

A sign was strung across the open space with a bold statement: "Congratulations Dr. Kerry!"

"What's all this?" Kerry was stunned. She waved to her mom and dad who stood amongst the community supporters in the crowd. Jesse's folks and brother Steve was there too.

"This, Kerry, is your new clinic." Jesse waved his hand around the room as the group looked on. He knew there was some risk in not including her in the decision about the location, but all things considered, it was convenient and best of all, paid for.

She looked around and tears rolled down her face. Kerry looked to Jesse, and he enfolded her in his embrace. She buried her face in his ribs.

"And, there's more." Jesse looked to Kerry's parents. Her mother smiled and nodded. Her father still hadn't caught on.

He slipped the small box from his jeans pocket and slid down to one knee. "Dr. Kerry Braun, vet of all things wild and keeper of my heart..." He paused to make sure she was paying attention. This was a lot of excitement in one night. "Will you marry me?"

With crocodile tears flowing down her face making rivers of dark mascara, she threw herself to him, nearly knocking him off his bended knee and shouted, "Yes, yes I will marry you!"

The video later went viral. Only then did she realize what a hot mess she was. Mrs. Braun, who was in on Jesse's plans, orchestrated the waving of a new banner that read 'Congratulations to the future Mr. and Dr. Davies'. Corks popped as plastic glasses and champagne were passed around. Mrs. Braun had prepared little desserts that were also making their way around the room. Someone ran to their car to get a blue tooth speaker, and the place filled with country music and chatter.

Kerry and Jesse, with friends in tow, wandered through the building. Kerry pointed out what would go in each room until she came to a room they hadn't previously discussed while dreaming about the clinic and drawing it out.

"Hey Jesse, this wasn't on the plans. What's this room?"

Jesse smiled and shuffled his feet self-consciously. "You'll have to have someplace to put up a playpen eventually, won't you? This is the back-office, nursing, childcare suite. Hope you like it."

"You think of everything!" Kerry was thrilled with this addition.

It had been a wonderful night. Friends and family congratulated the couple and thanked them for letting them be part of the night's fun. There was so much support in this community and the couple was immensely grateful. After everyone had gone and they were picking up the last of the party trash, Kerry smiled and shook her head.

"What's going on in your pretty head Dr. Braun, future Mrs. Dr. Davies?"

"You know I can't plan a wedding right now, right?"

"Yes, I know, and I've got some thoughts on that too." Jesse took her in his arms to soothe her angst. "We will save that for another day."

EPILOGUE

$\mathcal{S}$**teve**

    Steve watched from his place beside his little brother. They stood at a temporary altar on the edge of the Badlands in their full glory at sunset, with colorful drama building in the sky as the sun cast orange shadows across the carved hills in the background. Kerry walked up the dirt path toward Jesse, on the arm of her father. With each step of her cowgirl boots, a small cloud of Badlands clay dust formed a cloud at the hem of her satin wedding dress. He sniffed and looked at his own boots, willing the tears at the corner of his eyes to disappear.

It seemed like only yesterday he took a similar sacred walk to exchange vows with his late wife. Steve remembered it as a day of magic, fun and pure love. Vikki and Yvette planned every tiny detail, from the gowns and suits to the sunflowers and daisies woven in the flower girl's hair. A tear escaped onto the toe of his boot. Steve wiped the lingering evidence from the corner of his eye and looked at Jesse. It seemed like only yesterday they were fighting over childish things. Today was a magical day for a wedding.

As the reception wound down, Steve took inventory of his

family. Yvette and Dan danced to the final slow song, her shoes dangling over his shoulder, their faces gently pressed together. Chance had slipped into the house with his date and Stella was in the kitchen, helping the caterers and drinking wine. The bride and groom were saying farewell to parting guests.

Jesse and Kerry had a bright future ahead of them. Steve imagined they would have a family one day, when her veterinary practice was more established. Jesse would be a wonderful father. The kind of father Steve longed to be. Steve always saw himself as a family man; a dream shattered by illness and loss. He silently prayed for a second chance to find love and have a family.

ACKNOWLEDGMENTS

Special thanks to Linda Zeppa, mentor, intuitive, coach, and editor extraordinaire.

ABOUT THE AUTHOR

Kim Smart was raised on the edge of the Badlands in western South Dakota, but *grew up* in Alaska after landing there as a young nurse. Two decades later, she moved to San Diego to attend law school. After graduating, she returned to Alaska to again work in health care, this time at the intersection with law and public service.

Kim has always had a diverse love for writing and reading, enjoying romance, women's literature, historical fiction, poetry, and stories of people living authentic lives. Following a lifelong dream, Kim has turned to writing. She currently writes romance, women's literature, and historical fiction, along with nonfiction articles for various publications.

When not writing or traveling, Kim enjoys time with her parents and extended family, hiking and creating in the kitchen. She presently lives in Arizona, or wherever the wind blows her as she visits her children, grandchildren, and other interesting parts of our world. She has much to write about and many stories to tell!

Join Kim at https://kimsmartauthor to receive notice of new releases and exclusive reader giveaways.

ALSO BY KIM SMART

BUFFALO RIDGE RANCH SERIES

Two for Love - Book 2 (*Coming Spring 2020*)

Steve Davies lived his life in the shadow of his late wife's dreams. To emerge from his grief, he must take a chance. Hoping to expand the dreams they had together, he starts a dude ranch. In the process, he hires a cook - a city girl who brings along her son.

Bella Giordano needed to find safety for her young son. On a whim, she moves them from Manhattan to the Badlands of South Dakota, hoping the small town life, away from mob threats and smog, will be good for them both.

Will grief dissolve and a new opportunity be enough to build a new family?

The second novel in Kim Smart's Buffalo Ridge Ranch series sets the table for new opportunities and the possibility of love. Will hurts heal and love grow?

Taking Chances - Book 3 (*Coming Spring 2020*)

Chance Davies, champion bull rider, goes from being rock star of the rodeo to broken and lost after a final ride turns into a tragic accident. He is forced to return to Buffalo Ridge Ranch for recuperation after many years on the circuit. Through hard work and challenging himself, his body starts to heal. But will he allow his mind and spirit to heal and open up to new opportunities?

Sheltered from love, Pauline Whyte was always a misfit in the small town of Buffalo Ridge where everyone knew her family's business. She escaped the town gossip for a few years by moving away, only to have to return to care for her ailing father. Somehow, in this small town, love finds its way to her. Can she accept it?

To let love in, they must overcome loss and pain. Will her misfit ways fit into his new life for a happily-ever-after?

The third novel in Kim Smart's Buffalo Ridge Ranch series brings a story of overcoming the odds. Is that enough to find true love?

Dressing up Stella - Book 4 (*Coming Summer 2020*)

Stella Davies lived far away from Buffalo Ridge Ranch. Fearing repeat abandonment, she built the life of a cowboy nurturing her herd on the rugged edge of nature in Arizona. But to find happiness, she must face these fears. When she moves to the remote high desert, she is forced to face her fears.

Ranching was in Brandon Cage's blood, but a new career as a lawyer changed his focus. He buried himself in his new profession and totally ignored his heart's desires.

Do they have the gumption to clear the way to give love a chance? Will their love arrive in time to find a life happily-ever-after?

The fourth novel in Kim Smart's Buffalo Ridge Ranch series is about overcoming past hurts and prioritizing love.

STANDALONE NOVELS

Tangled Ribbons

The essences of individual humans are substantially more alike than they are different. Gertie Hall lives this truth as she rises from the young child of a Hitler henchman to a world-renown advocate for human rights. Through scientific endeavors, humanitarian efforts and a tireless fight to right the wrongs of her father, she explores her feminine self, intellect, ingenuity, and grit.

A hole remains in her soul where two childhood friends were ripped away, and Gertie's own father was complicit in the disappearance of their families. *Tangled Ribbons*, scene by scene, captures the life of Gertie, intertwined with the stories of her friends, Sarah and Hannah, who flee fiery Berlin and establish new identities and new lives in far away places. Late in their lives, Gertie offers a heart-wrenching plea for amends and a new generation is enfolded in their healing.

CPSIA information can be obtained
at www.ICGtesting.com
Printed in the USA
BVHW030546030920
587792BV00004B/186